When you grow up...

"I ain't goin to any goddam school, that's for sure. You though, you gotta go. You get your thang together, you could be like a real person, get like a job. You could have a cool car or at least a goddam wife or a kid maybe too."

"Who wants a goddam kid?" Ray said.

"I know. But when you get old, you start thinkin different."

"How you know?"

"I just know. Goddammit, I'll carry you one more year, then after that you ain't allowed to hang with me no more."

"Oh, so you're carryin *me*, is it?"

The boys eyed each other, smiled, punched each other. José lit up a cigarette, passed it to Ray.

Ray dragged. "What about you then?"

"What about me?"

"What you gonna do? With your life, I'm sayin. The rest of it."

"If I make it to twenty, I'll worry about it then."

OTHER BOOKS YOU MAY ENJOY

Black and White	Paul Volponi
Incarceron	Catherine Fisher
Jerk, California	Jonathan Friesen
The Orange Houses	Paul Griffin
Response	Paul Volponi
Rikers High	Paul Volponi
Secret Saturdays	Torrey Maldonado
Tales of the Madman Underground	John Barnes
Twisted	Laurie Halse Anderson

TEN MILE RIVER

PAUL GRIFFIN

speak
An Imprint of Penguin Group (USA) Inc.

SPEAK
Published by the Penguin Group
Penguin Group (USA) Inc., 345 Hudson Street, New York, New York 10014, U.S.A.
Penguin Group (Canada), 90 Eglinton Avenue East, Suite 700, Toronto, Ontario, Canada M4P 2Y3
(a division of Pearson Penguin Canada Inc.)
Penguin Books Ltd, 80 Strand, London WC2R 0RL, England
Penguin Ireland, 25 St Stephen's Green, Dublin 2, Ireland (a division of Penguin Books Ltd)
Penguin Group (Australia), 250 Camberwell Road, Camberwell, Victoria 3124, Australia
(a division of Pearson Australia Group Pty Ltd)
Penguin Books India Pvt Ltd, 11 Community Centre, Panchsheel Park, New Delhi - 110 017, India
Penguin Group (NZ), 67 Apollo Drive, Rosedale, Auckland 0632, New Zealand
(a division of Pearson New Zealand Ltd.)
Penguin Books (South Africa) (Pty) Ltd, 24 Sturdee Avenue,
Rosebank, Johannesburg 2196, South Africa

Registered Offices: Penguin Books Ltd, 80 Strand, London WC2R 0RL, England

First published in the United States of America by Dial Books,
a member of Penguin Group (USA) Inc., 2008
Published by Speak, an imprint of Penguin Group (USA) Inc., 2011

1 3 5 7 9 10 8 6 4 2

THE LIBRARY OF CONGRESS HAS CATALOGED THE DIAL BOOKS EDITION AS FOLLOWS:
Griffin, Paul, date.
Ten Mile River / by Paul Griffin.
p. cm.
Summary: Having escaped from juvenile detention centers and foster care, two teenaged boys live on their own in an abandoned shack in a New York City park, making their way by stealing, occasionally working, and trying to keep from being arrested.
ISBN: 978-0-8037-3284-1 (hc)
[1. Juvenile delinquency—Fiction. 2. Homeless persons—Fiction. 3. Runaways—Fiction.
4. New York (N.Y.)—Fiction.] I. Title
PZ7.G8813594Te 2008
[Fic]—dc22 2007047870

Speak ISBN 978-0-14-241983-0

Book design by Jasmin Rubero
Set in Goudy Old Style

Printed in the United States of America

for Kirby Kim and Nan Mercado

TEN MILE RIVER

1

RAY WAS BIGGER but José was boss. They were fourteen and fifteen, on their own and on the run.

José pulled two lead pipes from the knapsack he made Ray wear, slapped one into Ray's hand. "Shut your eyes before you smash the glass."

"You said the same damn thing last time."

"And you forgot to do it last time." José smacked the back of Ray's giant head.

They were hiding in the park. Ray studied the three-quarter moon spraying light they didn't need.

"Let's git to work," José said.

They made their way through the weed trees, downhill toward their target, a line of parked cars. José peeled off his shirt, wrapped it around his arm. He was skinny, ripped. "Strip off that shirt, Ray-Ray."

"I'm a'right." Ray's pipe slipped out of his sweaty hand, rang on the sidewalk. "Quit lookin at me like I'm a moron."

"You *are* a moron."

"Think I dropped it on purpose?"

"With you, you never know." José hustled ahead.

Ray eyed the tenements, the air conditioners hanging lopsided from windows. He worried one would fall someday, kill some kid in a stroller.

José never seemed to worry about what rotten thing might happen next. He gripped the pipe good, closed his eyes, swung down on an Escalade. The windshield imploded.

Ray smashed the far side of the street. There were a few jacked-up SUVs but mostly rear-ended Accords, gypsy hack Tauruses, poor folk rides. "Goddammit," Ray said. He knew he was breaking more than glass.

After they popped thirty-some windshields, lights and sirens spun a half mile up the road. The boys hid in the woods. José said, "That Escalade goes for eighty grand. All that bling, they deserve it."

They don't, Ray didn't say. Nobody does, not the poor folk, not the pimps neither. "Punks, every last one of 'em."

José poked Ray's gut. "A man's gotta eat, right, kid? Yo, after we get our bread, let's go boost us some DVDs. Gonna get me the *Goodfellas* deluxe."

"You got *Goodfellas* deluxe in your stack twice, still in the wrappers."

"Then I'm-a swipe me that other one," José said. "That

Godfather dude, homeboy never got his shirt on the whole movie. 'My name es *To*ny Mon*ta*na.' That Scarface was a first-rate thug, them model-lookin chicks hangin half-nekkid around that dope swimmin pool he got out back his mansion there." José leveled his window-breaking pipe Uzi style at Ray. "'Say hullo to my lil' friend!'" He purred *rat-a-tat-tat* as he sprayed Ray with invisible bullets.

Ray couldn't make the *rat-a-tat-tat* sound, came back with a lame *ka-click* as he mimed lock and load, gave José the gory glory he wanted.

José danced like Tony Montana gobbling up machine gun fire at the end of *Scarface,* the kingpin stoked on coke as if he'd sucked dry a generator big enough to power the city. Ray played along, body slammed the J-man. José flipped and pinned his boy, never mind Ray had J by four inches and seventy pounds. If life ever boiled down to a face-off Ray could check-'n'-deck the J-man in one throw. Not that Ray knew this yet.

"You got cut," José said.

"Scratch is all."

José grabbed Ray's arm, checked out the cut. "It's not bad."

"Gimme back m' arm."

"I tolt you to wrap yourself, kid. How come you ain't take off your shirt?"

Ray looked away, shrugged. "Was cold."

"*Right.* Idiot." José eyed Ray. "You did real good back there. Let's get paid."

◆

They worked their way through the woods to Van Cortlandt Park South and Jerry's Auto Glass, Best in The Bronx, the closest windshield fix for the thirty-some smashed cars. Jerry picked his teeth. " 'Sup boys?"

"You're up early, Jerry," José said.

"Thinkin I'm gonna be busy today." Jerry nodded at a banner strung over the garage bays: TODAY ONLY, 20% DISCOUNT.

"Might as well've had us put flyers under the windshield wipers," José said.

"Except there's no more windshields to put them flyers on, right, Slick?"

José nodded. "Howzabout our money?"

Jerry twirled his ear hair, sniffed his waxy fingers. "Howzabout how many?"

"Thirty-some," José said.

"That's good. Thirty-some shields is good." From a wad in his chest pocket Jerry flipped José a hundred.

"Buck fifty, we said," José said.

"See, here's the thing." Jerry took out his fake teeth to get rid of a string of food. "I'm short right now."

"You're short all the time," José said.

Jerry was short. He didn't like short jokes. "And you're funny, till I stab you."

"You stab me in a *dream* you better run," José said.

Jerry laughed, sounded like a car that couldn't get started. "You can't be fifteen, either of yous."

"I'm fifteen, yo. Ray's almost."

"He looks younger. Look at that head. Tweedle Dum. You a tard, Ray?"

Ray was a whiz kid, but he wasn't quick in the way of whipping off fast comebacks. He was slow smart. "Just lemme show you how retarded I am."

"Easy, Ray. Ray's a genius, Jerry. Ray fillets you for brains."

"Whatever. Frontin like you're sons of Gotti. I'd laugh except it's sad." Jerry laughed. "Go blow that hundred on your video games or whatever yous do, come back next week, maybe I got another gig. Yous worked, what, two minutes, scored a hundred bucks. You don't like it, go spot drugs, see how long yous last."

"We said a buck fifty." Ray stepped to Jerry with no aim of doing anything but stepping to Jerry.

"Chill, Ray. We see you soon, Jerry." José mimed a gun, popped a shot at Jerry.

"Next time I'm gonna make it up to you," Jerry said. "Thirty-some shields, huh? Nice. My daughter can go to Catholic school now. God bless you. I'll light a candle for yous." Jerry went into the shop to rinse his teeth.

"We oughta torch that punk's joint," José said.

"Gimme a gas can and a Zippo long neck, I'll do it." Ray didn't want to torch anything. He didn't want to pop windshields either, but a man had to eat. "A man's got to eat, dammit."

"Like I said," José said.

And a man has to stand by his brother, Ray didn't say. You survive foster care and juvie together, you stick by each other, you bet you do. Ray slugged José's shoulder.

José pulled Ray into a headlock. "Let's get us a grill and grill us some fish," José said.

"I'll grill it."

"You know you will." José laughed. He had a cool laugh, loud enough to wake the dark side of the world.

"Hell you laughin about, punk?" Ray laughed, had no idea why he was laughing.

José smiled a mouth full of perfect teeth. "He's callin me a punk now. Think you're tough, Ray-Ray?"

"I know I'm tough."

"The double Ray. The Ray-man. Kid Ray. Yeah, you might just be tough. But not as tough as me."

Ray didn't say anything.

"Ha!" José jumped Ray's back, made Ray carry him, played slap drums on his head. "Let's git us a grill, son."

They hopped a yard fence and stole a mini grill. On the subway south into Manhattan they flanked the grill, put on their gangster squints, dared the early-morning shift training in from The Bronx to say anything. An easy-to-make undercover cop boarded at 207th Street. "White boy tryin to front homeboy," José whispered.

The boys ditched the grill, slipped out of the train to the street. They bummed smokes from a nice old alcoholic so blind he didn't notice the boys were too young to smoke. They hunkered behind a Dumpster until two trains later when the 1 rumbled down the elevated track. They timed their run, hopped the turnstile, mixed with the morning rush into the head car. Tenement towers shadowed the train. "I wonder what's gonna happen to that grill now," Ray said. "It's kind of sad, if you think about it."

"Then don't think about it. Sad over a grill. Jesus, Ray. The cop'll boost it."

"I hope so. Sad to see it go to waste. That was a nice grill, that Weber."

"I don't give a damn about that grill. If the cop don't want it, it can ride itself all the way to the airport, let the bag handlers grill on it." José yawned.

Ray yawned. The yawns caught fire until the train punched out of the building shadows, swung a sharp bend of track into the morning glare, squealed over the rails.

Ray wondered at José asleep on his feet, his head resting on Ray's shoulder, a smile on the J-man's movie star face, no matter the train's squeal had shaken the other riders awake and ripped them from their dreams.

2

THEY HOPPED OFF the subway at 145th and hiked to Ten Mile River, a park in west Harlem. An elevated highway ran over the park and underneath the highway Amtrak rail. West of the tracks were ball courts and flatland to the Hudson River. East were wildwood cliffs leading up to Riverside Drive. José and Ray knew the way through the man-high weeds and pushed into the wildwood, lost to the world.

Hidden in junk trees midway up a cliff was a burnt-out stationhouse left over from the 1920s when the rails needed switchmen. Made of brick, the hut was good shelter, though the boys made it more than that. They'd used tin ripped off from gravel yard fences under the highway to patch the roof. A streetlight tap fed the air conditioner, heater, refrigerator, hot plate. Every appliance was street found except for the TV they stole from a delivery truck. A tap into the hub box of an apartment house uphill brought them premium channel cable. Listed MIA on the Children's Services roster, they didn't have to go to school, though they kept their school IDs for the odd hot shower they grabbed at the nearby rec center, free to students. All they needed was a little money for grub and the movies. As long as they kept a low profile they could do what they wanted, and they did.

José mostly tooled around on his trick bike and tried to be smooth with the chicks in the park. Shy Ray read. He had thousands of books and magazines, some from the garbage, most courtesy of the 82nd Street Barnes & Noble, which had a window that opened onto an alley. A kid could drop a book or five out the window into the street Dumpster. During the day Ray read how-to books and histories. At night he read spicy novels and mysteries to José, who couldn't read much more than the Micky D dollar menu. "All I need to know," he'd say.

As the boys approached the stationhouse, stray dogs materialized in the weeds. They mauled Ray and José with licking and whipping tails. The boys liked having the dumped pit bulls around. They were timid but looked vicious, kept squatters away from the house.

"A'right, dammit, let us in," José said to the dogs. "We saw 'em four hours ago and they're actin like we just come home from war. Them two scroungers is new."

"Nah," Ray said, "they was here before."

"Now I remember. They're the fair-weather friends. We run outta food, they run out with it."

"I like 'em," Ray said.

"I'd eat 'em if you'd let me. That one right there would feed us for a winter, the fat dope."

"He's funny, the fat dope one," Ray said. "I like him the most. C'mere, Fatty."

"Kissin the fat dope's filthy nose. Disgustin. You're sad, man. You're like a damn girl sometimes."

"What're you sayin now? I'll show you how much of a damn girl—"

"A'right, relax about it." José flopped onto his bunk, a half dozen dogs cuddling him. "Damn mutts." He kicked the dogs off the bed but they came back up. "Son, wake me when you get back from fishin and I'll help you cook the fish." José rolled over and fell asleep in a breath.

"Callin me a damn girl," Ray muttered. "Punk." He grabbed his reels, tackle and a book, skateboarded down to the river and set his lines. That done, he cut through the weeds, slipped through a rip in the chain link, dropped into the train tracks and wormed his way through the trackside trash to a car that had been boosted and torched. This was the boys' safe place for the odd times the cops parked alongside the woods or the pipe heads stumbled onto the stationhouse, hunkered there to cook up their methamphetamine. Now and then the junkies swiped the TV, easily replaced with an upgrade from a delivery truck with a weak padlock.

Ray pulled up the car's backseat. A cooler kept the bugs out of the candy bars, canned food, bottled water and whisky ends. Ray grabbed a fistful of M&M'S and headed back to the river. He lay back and read his book, the wind off the river hot. The book was about mind over matter. He had a bet running with José he would bend a spoon just by looking at it before the summer was out. Neither kid could remember what the stakes were. It was just *bet I can bet you can't bet I will bet you won't* by now.

Three hours later Ray had a bunch of porgies and a butterfish. He wrapped the fish in newspaper, whistled the dogs back from their high grass romping, skateboarded to the stairs that ran under the tracks and hiked the rest of the way uphill to the house. He shook José awake. "Yo, let's cook."

"Huh?" José looked at Ray as if he didn't know him.

"You wanted to cook it with me."

"Cook *what*?" José said.

"The fish."

"Right, the fish. You cook it and wake me when it's ready, the goddam fish." José rolled away for more sleep.

Ray went out back to cook the goddam fish. "Thank you, goddam fish," he said. He was sad now, but that was okay. It made him happy as hell, being sad as hell, he didn't know why. He figured he wasn't that sad anyway, gutted the fish and chucked the guts downhill. "I cook, I clean, I manage the dough," Ray said to the dogs. "I *am* like a damn girl."

The dogs cocked their heads. Anything Ray said thrilled them, especially when he was cooking up a fish fry. They were quiet and out of their minds with drool as they watched Ray soak the fish in butter and stick-cook it over open fire.

"Y'all relax." Ray crouched to let the dogs kiss him. "Buckets of bad breath slobber all over me now. Look at this mess." The train horn pulled Ray's attention west, where a tug bullied a gravel barge south. He imagined himself in the tug tower, not trolling the shallows as he and José sometimes did in their boosted rowboat, but far from shore in the fast current, riding a monster storm tide downriver into the bay, the ocean.

Ray had an urge to run away, except he had no idea where he wanted to go. More than that, what the hell would he do without José?

He winked at the dogs. "I could never leave y'all, don't worry. Not that y'all give a dag, whores, yessin me to death with kisses and licks and tail-waggin to get your fish." He chopped up a bunch of porgies, fed them to the dogs. He kicked the pig dogs off so the wimp ones could eat too. He went into the house and set the table. "Yo."

José snored.

"Git *up*." Ray yanked the window shade.

José pulled up his shirt to cover his eyes.

"Always takin off your shirt," Ray said. "Even in your sleep. You only wear a shirt to take it off. In the house, in front of the chicks in the park, anywhere. 'Ey, you hear what I'm tellin you?"

José snored.

"Narcissistic punk." Ray was sick at the sight of José's hair, long black loops braided perfectly into shiny cornrows. The J-man had perfect skin too, the skinny bastard. Husky Ray was zitty where he wasn't freckly, had lousy hair that frazzled and broke when he tried to cornrow it, dark red Brillo when sun-stroked. Ray kept his hair short and his shirt on.

He left the fish on a shelf out of dog reach for José and left. Halfway uphill Ray heard the door open behind him. In the door frame José scratched his armpit, yawned, "Yo, what up?"

"Lazy punk."

"Me?" José said. "Why I'm a lazy punk?"

"Y'all said you was gonna help me cook the goddam fish."

"Jesus, he's mad now. Look at 'im."

"Y'all better have them dishes cleaned up, the time I get back. Loafin around all your life, can't even pick up your own dag clothes off the floor."

"Son, that's the whole point of livin like this, no parents style," José said. "So I can leave my dag clothes on the floor. Pick up my clothes? Y'all lost your mind, yo?"

"Them dishes better be sparklin, yo. I'm serious, yo."

"Goddam girl, you are, yo."

"Fuck you, yo."

"*Jesus,* Ray. What's wrong, man? You a'right, man? C'mon back, man. Let's talk this out, brother."

"*Fuck* you."

"I don't get it," José said. "What's your problem all of a sudden?"

Ray didn't say what was his problem. He didn't know what was his problem. He was at the street now. He dropped his skateboard, pushed his giant body uphill.

José punched through the weeds after Ray. "Yo, where you goin, son?"

"Haircut."

"Again? Ha!"

"Shut up, man. Serious. I'll lay your shit out. No mood today."

"Ray, I jus playin wichou, dawg. C'mon home, son. Ray? Yo, Ray!"

Ray kicked his board up the Drive and sweat. On a muggy morning like this one he'd have loved to take off his goddam shirt.

3

RAY SKID-STOPPED IN front of Yolanda's Braid Palace, his once-a-week haircut spot. He popped his board off the street, caught it, told himself, "You are one cool motherfucker. Play this right and today's the day she's gonna let you kiss 'em. You can *do* this."

He was in love with Yolie's *tetas*, especially when she leaned them onto his shoulder to clip the top of his head. She wore tight T-shirts that went just halfway down her stomach, a sapphire stud in her belly button, tight jeans, brown lipstick, sparkly blue eye shadow. She smelled like cotton candy, vanilla and sometimes, when the day was hot, salt. Even though she was old, like forty or something, she was the most seriously fine woman in Washington Heights.

Ray figured Yolie loved him back a little, because why else would she stick her big brown breasts in his face when she was gelling down his ugly red hair? Then again, she stuck them in everybody's face. But Ray wasn't past taking charity teta. A man's gotta have dreams. He's gotta eat, dream the charity teta, maybe throw in a phat pair of sneakers, and the rest is gravy.

He parked his skateboard by the door, plopped into a folding chair and waited for Yolie with six other kids in love with Yolie's breasts. He pulled his *Scientific American* out of his back pocket and pretended to read an article about something called string theory but really he was checking out Yolie's booty. He waited until the other kids got their cuts and left, their hands in their front pockets to hide their chubbies. They didn't really love Yolie, not like Ray did. Ray dreamed not just of sexing Yolie up but of marrying her too. In the dreams he was saving her from tragedy, bandits raiding the wedding or a flood. Lots of slow-motion action scenes, his dream hair perfect, his dream body ripped, no need to wear a goddam shirt.

Gradually the string theory article pulled him in to the point where he forgot about Yolie, a feat as amazing as string theory itself, which suggested that down at their core, things weren't really made of anything. That atoms were nothing more than strings of energy. The guy who wrote the article thought this was cool. Ray didn't. "How's that possible? Nothing solid about life?"

"You talkin to me?" a kid leaving the shop said.

"You're up, amor." Yolie called everybody amor. She patted the salon chair.

Here we go. Kid Ray, you're the *dawg*. Be suave now. "'Lo, Missis Y-Yolie," he whispered, afraid to look Yolie in the eyes. He sat in the chair, his heart bashing his ribs. Somewhere in the last ten minutes the sky had turned black and puked a downpour of summer hail, and now the shop was empty except for Ray and Yolie. Ray didn't expect he'd survive this haircut. His heart was really slamming now. But what a way to go.

Yolie wrapped Ray in a smock. "Y'all know there's a barber shop across the street, right?"

"Yes ma'am."

"Okay. It's just, this is a braid shop, you know? I don't know how it got out that I cut hair. I ain't even licensed to cut hair."

"I don't mind."

"That's what the last kid said." Yolie's wristwatch alarm went off. "I gotta go to housin court, chico. You know how it is."

Dag, Ray thought. "I'll come back later."

"No no, you stay. This one is free if you let my niece practice on your head. She's up from the island, cut heads down there. She real good."

"Um, *gracias, Señora Yolie, pero está bien*." Ray hopped out of the chair.

"Sit." Yolie pushed Ray back down with her hands some but mostly with her breasts. Ray caved into the chair. Yolie yelled to the back of the shop, "Amor, y'all finish up the bookkeepin later. I got a sweetie pie waitin on a haircut here." She mussed Ray's head, made for the door. "That gorgeous red hair, so thick. I don't know why you won't let it grow. We could roll it to dreads and put red bead shells in it."

Ray imagined how long hair and red bead shells would make him look. He figured he'd look pretty much the same, fat, except with long hair and red bead shells. He was sweating under the plastic smock. He closed his eyes and dreamed of Yolie. She was kissing him on the mouth, caressing his neck—

She caressed his neck. Ray opened his eyes to the mirror and saw behind him a girl, fifteen, maybe even sixteen. She wasn't really caressing his neck but dusting it with powder before she put the paper towel around it. "Hi."

Hi, Ray almost said, his voice lost who knew where but nowhere he could find it for speaking use. This chick was too beautiful. She was like Yolie but young. She even smelled the same. Her hair was long black loops. Her eyes were black.

"How you want me to do it?" she said.

"Huh?"

"Your head."

"My head?"

"Maybe the same but shorter?"

"Um, the same but shorter."

She went to work on Ray's head. "You're funny-lookin kind of."

"I am so."

She laughed. She had a great laugh, loud and warm like goddam José's. "That came out bad," she said. "Like, you look like you'd be funny, I mean."

"I'm like not that funny, though."

She laughed through her nose, cut Ray's hair. "Hold still, sweetie pie."

You did not *just call me sweetie pie,* he almost said. Yolie called him sweetie pie all the time, but that was an old lady saying it. This was a real chick saying it now. Oh. My. God.

The girl spun the chair so that Ray faced her. "You a'right? Your head's turnin all red and you're breathin funny. You havin a heart attack on me?"

"Swallowed my. Gum. It'll pass. Don't worry, no need to break out the defibrillator just yet."

"What?"

"No, like I'm sayin I won't go into cardiac arrest on you, you gotta start the cardiopulmonary resuscitation."

"You a smart-type dude, huh?"

"Psh, nah."

"Yeah, then what's this?" She grabbed the magazine he'd rolled into his hand. "*Scientific American,* eh? String theory? Most boys your age be readin *Hustler.*"

"I read *Hustler* too."

The chick winked. "I got the feelin you're one of those brainiacs, tries to hide it so your boys don't give you bad play. It's in your eyes."

His eyes? *Her* eyes. He wanted to speak differently with her, to use almost proper English, maybe even half-decent grammar, God help him. He couldn't speak, his tongue stuck to the roof of his mouth. He chewed his gum to work up some saliva to unglue his tongue.

"Came back up, huh?" the chick said.

"Huh?"

"The gum you, ahem, swallowed."

Shit. "Can't keep a good gum down." Do not talk anymore. Do, not, be, a, loser. For five seconds. Try.

She offered her hand for a shake. "Trini."

Ray stared at this Trini chick's hand. He'd never touched a woman before except for when he'd accidentally bump into one in the crowded street or when one cut his hair, and those times he knew the chick was just touching him because she had to. But here this chick wanted to touch him, to hold his clammy overgrown paw. "Trini?"

"That's my name," Trini said.

Ray nodded as he shook Trini's hand. Static electric shocks numbed his fingers. He wondered if she felt them too.

"I don't suppose you have a name?" she said.

"Yup."

Trini laughed an aria. "What is it then, your tag?"

"Ray. Mond."

"Mond? That's a slick last name, boy. Ray *Mond,* James *Bond*. P.S., you *seen* that new Bond boy? He's *off, the, hook fine,* ohmygod."

"No, I mean like R-Raymond. All one word."

"Oh, *Ray*mond!"

That laugh. That music. Them eyes. Ray's legs shook. He was going to wet himself. "I got to go to the can."

"Go 'head, sweetie pie. It's in the—"

"I know, thanks." He'd only tossed off in there a hundred times while waiting for haircuts. He ran to the bathroom, his legs so shaky he had to sit to pee.

JOSÉ WAS WORKING the Grand Theft Auto stick when Ray kicked in the door, his arms full of supplies, a hundred bucks worth of Cap'n Crunch, roach spray, dog food, cigarettes, scratch tickets, and Hershey's syrup. Ray dropped the stuff to the floor, sank down against the wall. "My life is over."

"Whatever happened to *Hi honey I'm home*?"

"You gotta see her. She's so fine she makes your guts squish."

"Whatever that means. And that's what you said about that chick what bags groceries at the bodega. Woman won't even let us steal gum, selfish hag."

"J, look at me. This is serious. She's *Playboy* pretty."

José spun from the TV to Ray. "Where she at?"

"Yolie's."

"Tt, Yolie." José spun back to the TV, worked the joystick, killed two guys with head shots. "Hell, son, I seen that old lady. She ain't all that."

"Not her. She got a niece."

José spun back to Ray. "You're messin up my game here."

"She's better-lookin than Miss Febs. Last year's calendar."

José dropped his joystick and all interest in the video game. "I'm gonna ride all the way up there in the rain and I'm not gonna wanna kill you when I see her? Dag. Then let's go."

"Now?"

"No, next year. Grab your board."

"Lemme grab my board then."

"I just said that." José rummaged his clothes pile, did the sniff check on a shirt, decided it passed, headed out and uphill.

Ray looked at the fat dope dog that had settled at his feet to slobber all over its paws. "Why'd I do that, Fatty? Why'd I tell him? Now she's gonna fall in love with him. She liked me, man. She thought I was smart. I'm a goddam idiot."

"Yo Ray!"

"Comin, dammit!"

Yolie's was closed, the door sign flipped to WE'LL BE BACK AT . . . and then there was a paper clock that had lost its hands. The hail stopped and left behind a muggy-ass drizzle.

José took off his shirt, wiped the rain off his trick bike.

"Wipin down his bike with his goddam shirt. It's okay to *wear* your shirt once in a while too," Ray said. "They got rags for the bike wipe."

"Then you got a *rag* on you, *Mom*?" José ran his fingers over the nicks he'd earned during his overcareful, twenty-eight-minute shave that morning. He was shaving goddam near once a week now.

Ray shaved once a month. He didn't need to. He fussed with a zit.

"Let's swipe us some cold beer," José said.

"Let's."

They swiped beer, coasted double on José's trick bike down the Drive to Ten Mile River and crashed the bike in the high grass. They drank and José fell asleep.

Ray lay back and watched the last clouds hustle east. The breeze picked up and bent the grass over him. The sun was strong but the air had dried out. Seeing this peacefulness, Ray got the feeling he was on the edge of understanding something big, but he didn't get past being on the edge. He sipped his beer, drifted, slept, dreamed of the Trini chick. She was putting her hand into his shorts—

He woke up, José's finger poking at the bulge in his shorts. Ray stood up fast. "Yo, get off, man. The fuck? Yo, this ain't juvie, son."

"You're funny, Ray-man. You're yellin at me and you're still hard, man."

"Am not either. That's normal."

José fell over laughing, thrashed in the high grass. "'That's normal,' he says. Then we gotta put you out to stud, homie. That or the circus. *Check it out check it out check it out, Boner* Man! G'head, homeboy. Tame that snake. Go do what you always do ten times a day, 'Yeah, I'm-a go check out the *river,*' he always says. 'Be back in like five minutes.' Ha!"

"Yeah, and what about you, all them trips to the woods. 'Gonna go pitch a stool.' Right. Bringin your *readin* material with ya. Can't even read, ya bastard."

"Don't need to know how to read to git the gist of Miss Febs's story."

"Pokin my package. Hell is wrong with you, man?"

"Look at the way he's lookin at me," José said. "Yo, I'm a proven matador, man. I *been* with chicks. You ain't even kissed one."

"You ain't been with chicks, lame-ass liar."

"Have so. I even sucked titty. I got milk."

"Look at this bullshit artist. A chick got to be pregnant to lactate."

"Lackate?" José said.

"Make milk. Or else she got to have just birthed a kid."

"No she *don't.*"

"I read it in a book."

"Damn readin," José said. "Really? Maybe it was my spit

mixin with the baby powder she sprinkled into her bra."

"Maybe it was her roll-on, you was suckin her *arm*pit. Breast milk, he says. Li. Ar."

"I tolt you, that one chick who works the ice cream truck with her pops, that time I helped her wash the truck, I sucked her titties for like at *least* twenty seconds."

"You sucked your *mama's* titties for twenty seconds," Ray said.

"I sucked *your* mama's titties and made her take me shoppin after." José sucker punched Ray, a gut shot.

Ray body slammed the J-man. They rolled themselves filthy in the riverside clay. José wiped himself off. "Hoo... Dag, I ain't laughed like this since yesterday."

"Yeah."

"Yeah."

The boys caught their breath. José slapped the back of Ray's head. "How much money we got, kid?"

"None."

"Sounds about right. Let's go get us some money and hit the flicks, Ray-Ray."

"Sounds about right. Y'all keep your hands to yourself from now on."

"Relax, son. You kill me, you just about do."

5

"BACK SO SOON?" Jerry said. The shop was cranking, new windshields going up assembly line style.

"Buck fifty this time, Jerry, and I mean it." José folded his arms.

Jerry laughed. "Kid, you gotta wait a while before you pop more shields. People'll get suspicious."

"No they won't. We'll do the other side of Gun Hill, you know, Woodlawn, over by the seminary. Right, Ray?"

"Cemetery," Ray said.

"Nah nah," Jerry said. "They got too many shops over by Gun Hill Woodlawn for anybody to come down to my place. Nah look, come back next week."

"C'mon man, we gotta see the new *Spider-Man*. Give us twenty bucks."

"Yous kill me, you know that, right? Yous frickin slay

me. The movies they gotta see now. Frickin Spidey." Jerry sucked his teeth, squinted at the boys. "Tell yous what. Here." He flipped them a fifty. "That's a tip there for yous, for this mornin."

José took. He looked at Ray. Ray shrugged.

"Yous don't say thanks?"

"Way I see it," José said, "that's what you owe us."

"You kids are too much. 'Ey, c'mere." Jerry took them into his greasy office, shut the door. "Yous wanna make some real money?"

"As opposed to fake?" Ray said.

"Round Face, calm down, okay? I'm tryin to tell you something here."

"Tell it," José said.

"You know how all the pimps park on the park there, by Jerome Ave?"

"We seen 'em."

"You see the same cars there, right, night after night, maybe not in the same exact spot but close, right, a block north, south, either way, right? Tonight go pick out a new Escalade or a Navigator, you know, somethin that goes like eighty, eighty-five long, like all souped up."

"We know what you mean," José said. "Yeah?"

Jerry winked. "Keep an eye on it. Get to know where it lives night to night. The coast is clear, you're gonna grab the VIN number. It's by the registration sticker, on the dash. You can see it through the windshield. Bring me the number, I'll have my girlfriend dress real nice. She—"

"I thought you was married," Ray said.

"I am." Jerry looked from Ray to José. "What's his problem?"

"Never mind him," José said. "Keep goin. Your galfriend dresses nice—"

"She goes to the Lincoln dealer, bats eyes, bumps the counter with her double Ds, tells them she lost her key, she gives them the VIN, they cut her a new key, I give yous the key, yous boost the car nice and easy."

"We can't—"

"Hold up, Round Face, lemme finish. Yous're Joe Citizens drivin all nice, right, speed limit, stop signs, lights all perfect, right, yous wear a shirt and slacks at the waist, right, no monkey pants and prison tees, okay, no crazy nigger stuff here."

Ray chewed the inside of his cheek.

José winked. "We don't drive crazy nigger style, Jerry. We don't drive period."

"You do now. C'mon, I'll give yous lessons."

"I'm fifteen," José said. "He's fourteen."

"In the back of the lot here, nobody's gonna see. C'mon, you and your boy Round Face here, I'll have you boys ready to race NASCAR before the week is out. All yous gotta do is get from Jerome to the shop, what, a mile max."

"Let's go, man." Ray started for the door.

"Wait." José squinted at Jerry. "How much, for the Lincoln?"

"Buck fifty, and I won't short you."

José laughed and walked. "C'mon, Ray."

"Wait, wait, c'mere," Jerry said. "Okay. I'll give yous a grand."

"Each," José said.

Jerry laughed and walked.

"Where you goin, Jerry? This is your office. Eight hundred each," José said.

"I'll give yous fifteen hundred, split it how you like. We'll do a car a month. Who wants to drive first?"

A week passed, they both knew how to drive. José went to steal them nice clothes. Ray went to get a haircut.

The Braid Palace was packed. Yolie looked tired but smiled and called everybody amor anyway. For twenty minutes Ray tried to make himself get out of his chair to go talk to Yolie, but each time he almost got up, he leaned back and pretended to read a computer magazine he found in the trash can. Then he got a chubby and had to stay in the chair, figured he'd read until his chub went away, settled in for the long haul, read an article by this guy at MIT, said that eventually humans won't need biological bodies, that our brains will be computer code, our bodies computer chips, that we'll be able to e-mail ourselves across the universe, and that's when we'll know for sure God doesn't exist.

This bummed Ray out.

He tossed the magazine. Chubber gone, he forced himself to walk through the waiting area to the salon chair where Yolie was clipping a kid. "Missis Yolie?"

"Amor?"

"Like I see how busy you are, and if you want I could get a clip from, like, Trini."

"You don't mind?"

"She did a real good job last time." She really didn't. Ray had a divot in the back of his head.

Yolie squinted at the divot, blinked, looked at the full waiting room, sighed, nodded. "Trini, amor?" she called to the back of the shop, where Trini was rolling a woman's head down to braids. "I got a sweetie pie waitin on a haircut here."

"I'm almost done, Tía." Trini looked out from behind the privacy screen. When she saw Ray she giggled.

Ray tossed the chick a superslick nod, like he didn't give half a damn about her. You are *Ray Mond,* he told himself. You are seriously the shit.

He leaned on an empty salon chair that spun out from under him, slipped into a pile of clipped hair.

Yolie turned away and exploded, her great tetas shaking as she laughed. Trini looked up at the ceiling and howled. She had the cutest teeth. They were kind of buck. Trini winked at Ray. "Hello, Mister Mond."

Ray nodded and sat in the salon chair. Face red, lips tingling, he prayed for death.

◆

The J-man was watching the *Scarface* DVD. He was saying Tony Montana's lines with Al Pacino. His imitation was spot on, perfect Cubano accent. "Sani*ta*tion? Sani*ta*tion? I tol' you to say sani*tarium*."

Ray snuck into the stationhouse, crept on top of the couch arm, sucker slammed the J-man, World Wide Wrestling cage match style. He almost got a fart off on the J-man's head.

José flipped Ray, farted on his face. "Whoa, hold still. You got like no hair now."

"That's the style."

"Sure it is, in the mental hospital. Was she there?"

"Phew, man, you reek."

"Baloney an' Cap'n Crunch sammich. Look at that head. She better be pretty, Ray, 'cause she can't cut hair worth a lick. You got divots all up the side your dome. You look retarded, man, like you oughta be wearing a helmet when you walk around. You look like you fell off a bike."

The Fatty dog burped in his sleep, his butt on José's pillow.

"Git off my pillow, man." José kicked the dog off his bed.

The dog went to Ray's bunk and slept on Ray's pillow. Ray petted the dog.

"Goddam dog," José said. "He can't go out and play with the rest of the dogs? Goddam two of you, I don't know what I'm gonna do." José threw Ray his new duds.

Ray dressed. The clothes were tight. "Whattaya think?"

"Ray, serious man, you gotta wear a hat. You look like you're out on a day trip."

"You don't shut up about my hair I'll kill you in your sleep, man."

"I'd have to be asleep for you to kill me."

Ray checked his head in the cracked mirror. "I like it like this."

"You better, because that mess is gonna take a while to right itself. You gonna be livin with that head a *lonnnng* time."

They got into a slap fight, laughed themselves tired, went to sleep in their clothes, José setting the alarm clock he'd stolen that afternoon for two in the morning. The Fatty dog hogged the bed in his sleep, kicked Ray onto the floor. Ray let the dog have the bed. The dog snored louder than José. Ray couldn't sleep, watched the gangster movie on mute. As he drifted off into dreams of Trini, Scarface was about to die.

Three in the morning up in The Bronx they hunkered in the bushes skirting the park and Jerome Avenue. Overhead the trees swayed with a hot wind. José kept a lookout for the Navigator that parked here about this time. "I gotta piss." He hustled off into the woods.

Ray pulled a spoon from his pocket, balanced it on his index finger and stared at it like Superman melting steel with his eyes. The background stole his focus from the spoon. Across the street were tenements bombed with graffiti bright in the streetlight. Somebody had hit a nearby mailbox with a fat Day-Glo perma-marker. The ink said:

NOBODY CARES ABOUT YOU.

"Aw no. Some little kid's just learnin to read, spells it out real slow? Nuh-uh." Ray scratched at the graffiti with his spoon.

"Will you quit babblin with yourself?" Back from the bramble, José ripped the spoon from Ray's hand, chucked it into the woods, slapped Ray's head. "Freak. What are you doin?"

"Till you chucked m'spoon I was, like, spoon bendin."

"You was chippin at that mailbox with it, raisin noise to tell the world we're out here. Quit lookin after that dag spoon. Look here for a sec."

"What?"

"You're almost fifteen now, punk. You can't be actin like a kid no more."

"I ain't no kid."

"You're a goddam kid. Jerkin off up at that Braid Palace all the time with your retard haircuts, talkin to yourself, scratchin mailboxes, rollin around on the floor with them damn dogs every chance you get, talkin to 'em like they have a goddam idea what you're sayin, in love with a new chick ever' other week but you ain't got the balls to drop a hi on a one of 'em. That's kid shit, straight up. Quit poutin.

I'm puttin my feet down this time, you're goin a school come fall."

"This bullshit again."

"I'll kick your fat butt all the way there if I got to, Ray."

"Then you're comin with me."

"I ain't goin to any goddam school, that's for sure. You though, you gotta go. You get your thang together, you could be like a real person, get like a job. You could have a cool car or at least a goddam wife or a kid maybe too."

"Who wants a goddam kid?" Ray said.

"I know. But when you get old, you start thinkin different."

"How you know?"

"I just know. Goddammit, I'll carry you one more year, then after that you ain't allowed to hang with me no more."

"Oh, so you're carryin *me,* is it?"

The boys eyed each other, smiled, punched each other. José lit up a cigarette, passed it to Ray.

Ray dragged. "What about you then?"

"What about me?"

"What you gonna do? With your life, I'm sayin. The rest of it."

"If I make it to twenty, I'll worry about it then." José nodded toward the fire hydrant across the street. "Here he comes."

The Lincoln Navigator docked in front of the hydrant. The driver got out, stretched, blip-blipped his automatic key at the car, the locks clunked. He went inside a building down the block.

José pitched the cigarette, dropped his arm over Ray's shoulder. "Y'all ready?"

They swiped deep breaths, checked the street and made for the car. José sank the copy key, opened the door. Ray jumped in and popped the glove compartment with his backup spoon. He ripped the alarm wire out before the alarm beeped three times. The street was quiet.

"Attaboy, Ray-Ray."

"Tomorrow we gotta come back and spray-paint over that mailbox thing."

"Hell you talkin about?"

"That Nobody Cares About You ink."

José rolled his eyes, rolled the ignition, drove away while Ray scanned the streets for cops. The streets were dead.

José drove the car into the garage. Jerry pulled down the door. Something curbside caught Jerry's eye, a traffic cop sticking a bright orange ticket under the windshield blade of Jerry's Mercedes parked in front of a dead fire hydrant. "Four in the mornin and she's peelin oranges." Jerry limped outside, José and Ray on his tail. He waved to the cop driving away in her cruiser, his hand going from five fingers to one as she rounded the corner. He snatched the ticket, walked it to the car parked behind him, stuffed the ticket under that car's windshield blade. "Think they'll pay it?"

"I look like a fortune-teller?" José said.

"Sometimes you get a nigger doesn't read the ticket, he pays it."

"Jerry," Ray said, "you blind?"

"What?" Jerry said. "Yous ain't *nigger* niggers. Yous're Porda Ricans, right?"

"Never mind that now," José said. "I'm more wonderin if you gonna pay us, Jerry."

"Relax." Jerry peeled off fifteen hundreds and slapped them into José's hand. He nodded. "Yous done real good. We'll do another one next month."

José looked at the money. He looked at Ray. Ray nodded. José stuffed the money into Ray's pocket. Ray patted his pocket. "Now that's real money," he said.

Jerry laughed. "Frickin Round Face. You kill me, kid."

José and Ray walked off.

Jerry said, "'Ey."

"What," both said.

"I'm proud of yous."

José and Ray looked at Jerry as if he'd cursed them in a language they didn't know. They looked at each other. Ray shrugged. They left.

"Frickin kids," Jerry said.

Back at Ten Mile, Ray wrestled the dogs. "Look at Fatty, man. He's like human the way he looks at you. Look."

"Hell you sayin now?" José sipped his celebration beer,

worked the clicker to pull up the on-screen TV guide. "Y'all are drunk, kid."

"The other dogs, you call 'em, they turn their whole head to look at you. But Fatty, you call him, he just turn his eyes."

"Do not."

"Watch. Yo Fatty."

The dog did what Ray said it would do.

"See," Ray said, "he's human, man."

"Then put him outside, then. I don't want no human dogs in my house."

"He can sleep with me."

"He *should* sleep with you." José squinted at the dog, at Ray. "You're a little crazy, I'm thinkin, Ray."

"I might be."

"Y'all stop readin so much. Freakin me out. Human dogs, of all the strangenesses. That readin is gonna be the death of us."

Ray laughed. "Hell're you talkin about now?"

"I don't goddam know." José clicked off the TV, flopped back in his bunk. "Night."

"Night yourself."

"Night yourself back at you. Git offa me, dogs. The stink, man. Phew. Dog stew, we should make." José went straight to snoring.

The sun was almost up. Ray lay back, using the Fatty dog for a pillow. He patted the fifteen hundred bucks in his pocket, whispered, "We're rich."

6

RAY WATCHED THE *abuelita* fix the flowers. "Could you put a little more of that angel's hair or whatever in?"

"The baby's breath?" the florist said. "You want more? I put a lot in already."

"Okay."

"You don't want it to overwhelm the roses. *Me entiendes, hijo?* No, I mean, you want me to, I'll put more."

"Nah, it's okay," Ray said. "I don't want it to overwhelm the roses."

"That's right." The florist pounded her cash register. "Two dozen extra-long stem comes to a hundred and sixteen sixty . . . gimme a hundred and we good."

Ray paid, stuffed the roses into his knapsack but they didn't fit. "I borrow your scissors there?"

"Huh?" The woman gave Ray her scissors.

Ray cut the stems down to half and the roses fit in his knapsack. The florist's cheeks turned white. Ray put the scissors back on the counter. *"Gracias, señora."*

The old woman sat down and mopped her brow with a perfumed cloth.

Ray kicked his skateboard past Yolanda's Braid Palace thirty-one times. He stopped at the corner, opened his knapsack and dumped the roses into the trash can. He rode away downhill, spun back, kicked his board uphill to the trash can, pulled the roses out of the garbage and gave them to a strung-out hooker clicking her heels and snapping Bubble Yum on the corner.

The hooker cried. Ray wasn't sure if the hooker was a girl or a guy or a girl-guy, but it didn't matter. Ray liked all hookers as a matter of principle, even though he'd never been with one. He gave the hooker a hundred dollars. "You too young, chico," the hooker said. She was a guy, Ray could tell now.

"No, I mean, you just keep it," Ray said.

"Say what?"

Ray kicked his skateboard past The Palace. Yolie smoked a cigarette, fanned herself with a magazine as she talked on the phone. Her nipples were hard under her shirt. Ray turned around and went to the hooker.

"Take the money back," the hooker said. She was crying really hard now.

"Um, nah, but could I have like half the roses back?"

Yolie scratched her armpit, squinted at Ray. "You just got cut yesterday, no?"

Ray gulped. "I . . . know."

"Amor, c'mere." Yolie took Ray by the hand, brought him to the kitchen. "Sit."

"Yes'm."

She poured him a Coke, felt his face with soft hands. "You're warm." She took a thermometer out of the cabinet, rinsed it. Ray hated thermometers as a rule because he knew that after folks used them the first time they forgot whether they were mouth or ass, but with Yolie it was okay. Yolie would never stick an ass thermometer in your mouth. She stuck the thermometer in Ray's mouth. "You're runnin a little hot."

"I ain't slept is all."

"How come?"

Ray shrugged. He opened his knapsack, took out the roses. "They're for, like, you, but for Trini too, also."

Yolie nodded. "They're real pretty. Thank you." Yolie put her hand over her mouth. Her tetas shook as if she stood on quaking ground. "Lemme get Trini then," she said through her fingers.

Ray panicked. "You don't gotta."

"Sit." Yolie boobed Ray back into the chair, hit the stairwell that went to the upstairs apartment.

Ray sweat. Nothing happened for two minutes except the room got fifty times hotter. Ray shivered.

"Hi." She wore a pink half shirt, low-rider jeans, sunshine patches at the pockets. She moved in slow motion, floated as she came down the stairs.

"Yup," Ray said. "Hi, I mean."

"Mister Mond, you do ka-*rack* me up."

"I, like, you wanna rocks chuck—guh, go chuck rocks in the river with me?"

The minute he opened the stationhouse door for her he thought, *Why* am I doing this? Why'd I bring her here?

The music loud, José didn't hear them come in. He was watching TV, golf, his hand in his pants, not moving, just there.

Ray cleared his throat.

José eyed Trini, jumped, smoothed his hair. "We got company, I see."

"This is Trini," Ray said. He wanted to weep.

José nodded at Trini, no big deal. "What up."

"What up."

The dogs slobbered all over Trini. She cuddled them. "Mutt lovers, huh?"

José shrugged.

"He wants to eat 'em. *I'm* a dog lover, though," Ray said.

Trini hadn't heard Ray. She was all about smooching the dogs. "Look at these cuties."

"Sad thing about dogs?" José said.

"Yeah?" Trini said.

"Folks take old dogs and grind 'em up for horse food."

"It's the other way *around*," Ray said, but he might as well have not been there. Trini and José pretended they weren't checking each other out. "Killin dogs for food," she said. "That's *hor*rible."

"I know," José said. "I read it in a book somewheres. Breaks my heart." José sighed.

Ray rolled his eyes.

José grabbed a magazine to fan himself, didn't realize the mag was *Playboy*.

Trini noticed. She laughed.

"Hot day," José said.

Don't you goddam do it, Ray almost said.

"It's not that hot," Trini said.

"Phew." José took off his shirt.

He goddam did it.

Trini eyed the J-man's ripped abs, caught herself, looked away, got back to the business of playing with the dogs, but the damage was done. The J-man's eight-pack: The atomic bomb had been dropped.

Ray moped to his bunk, fussed with the fat dope dog. Fatty didn't want to play, ditched Ray, hit the couch to sleep in peace. Now Ray couldn't do anything but watch José show Trini around, show her the gigantic TV that split-screen, cartoons big box, Yankees game little. Ray poured Trini a Coke.

"Thank you, Raymond."

"Raymond?" José said. "Who's *Raymond*?"

Ray flipped off José behind Trini's back.

Trini ran her hand over the bookcases. "Y'all are set up good here, huh? Cool clubhouse."

"Clubhouse?" Ray said. "This is our *house* house."

José shot eyes at Ray.

"Wait, for real, you guys like *live* in this place?" Trini said. "You can't live here. Where's your folks?"

"Don't got 'em," Ray said.

"Don't want 'em," José said. "Where you from? You Dominican?"

"From the island, but I'm born here."

"Boricua, huh? I like Boricuas."

"Boricuas are my favorite," Ray said.

"Y'all live here on your lonesome," she said. "Dag."

Ray watched her take in the messy stationhouse, the crummy makeshift kitchen, the decaying walls, holes in the floor, the tin roof, the street-found furniture, the duct tape that held together what was left of the windows, her eyes ending on them, the boys. "Is this legal, livin like this?"

"Well—" Ray said.

"We're emaciated minors," José said. "Why you ain't back in Puerto Rico?"

"I'm back here for school. Can't believe y'all have no folks."

"You come back *here* for school?" José said.

"I got this thing where they like pay my way at this private downtown."

Ray ached. He *knew* she was smart.

"White folks' school, huh? That's chill. They ain't all bad." José licked his lips and rubbed his goddam skinny stomach. "You hungry?"

"I'm okay," Trini said.

"C'mon, we'll take you out," José said.

"Nah, that's okay."

"Serious," José said. "You wanna come to Micky D's wif us? Today be twofers on the dollar menu. Micky makes a mean chimichanga."

"Um, I have like fifty cents on me."

"We look poor to you?" José said. "We always pay our lady friends' ways."

"We always do too," Ray said. "That's a rule of ours."

"You're like sixteen, right?" José said.

"Yeah, I'm like sixteen."

"I'm like almost sixteen," José said. "Ray's gonna be like fifteen in two months."

"A month and a *half*."

"Right, right." José held the door for Trini. "Yeah, so let's go."

"I thought you had to be sixteen to be emancipated," Trini said.

"Fourteen. New law." José smiled. "Lucky for us, right?"

Ray side-eyed José.

"I'm worried about y'all," Trini said. "On your lonesome and all."

José put his arms over Trini's and Ray's shoulders. "We ain't lonesome."

At McDonald's José ran into a kid who owed him money. He chased the kid across the Broadway rush. Stuck on the far side of traffic, Ray lost José in the crowd.

"What happened there?" Trini said.

"He was tryin to catch up with a friend."

"Uh-huh. He's interesting, that José of yours. How y'all hook up?"

"He's my brother."

"For real?"

"Yup, just not by blood."

"Pals, huh?"

"Friends to the ends, just don't tell him I said that."

"I won't. That's nice, though." She strung her arm through Ray's, pals style.

Ray stared at her arm in his. "So, like, you want a Superfry?" he said to her arm.

"Okay," she said. "After, you show me the river."

They sat in the hollow of a wild oak curling out of the riverbank. Ray fed his fries to the squirrels. "Normally we don't let girls in the house, but, you know, since me and your aunt are friends and all."

"Sure, sure, can't be havin girls in the house,"Trini said.

"Well, it's just the place smells bad on account of the dogs, and we don't want girls thinkin it's us that smell, because the dogs, they're sneaky like that. They make a smell by you and then they leave and then the girl thinks you made the smell."

"Well, I didn't think it smelled *that* bad."

"Really? Thank you. I like really appreciate that."

Trini's smile waxed, waned. She fed bits of fries to a seagull. "Y'all don't get scared in there at night, that stationhouse?"

"Nah. Psh."

"Isn't it like illegal, not goin to school?"

Ray looked away. "You like school?"

"I love school. Why they call this place Ten Mile River?"

"Because it's ten miles up from the southern tip of the island."

"Okay."

"That's what I read, anyway. I don't mean to sound cocky or anythin, like I'm this *reader* or somethin. Like I don't mean to sound like I know what I'm talkin about."

"You don't, don't worry."

"Thanks," he said. "Yeah."

"You are a funny boy."

He had a whole list of cool questions to ask her but forgot them. Those buckteeth killed him. "So, can you bend spoons?"

"Huh?"

"Forget it. So, you like my homeboy?"

Trini squinted, wrinkled her nose at Ray.

"He's real handsome, right?"

"He's okay."

"You like him, right?"

"He's okay."

"Okay. I could, like, tell him you like him if you want me to."

"Nah, nah, nah, that's okay," she said.

"Only if you wanted me to, I'm sayin."

"Nah."

"It's an open-ended offer."

"Okay."

"So, you want me to tell him then?"

"Nah."

"Okay, you let me know."

"Okay."

"Does that mean—"

"I'll let you know, Raymond, okay?" She munched a fry. "I do think it's nice that he looks out for you, though. He seems sweet. He'd have to be to be one of your boys." She looked at Ray, smirked. "He a ladies' man though, right? Your boy a player?"

Ray smiled.

She studied Ray, his eyes. "Seriously, you're mad smart, right? All those books. You're different."

“Nah, nah, I’m just your regular old fat giant type of ugly dope kid.”

She slapped his leg. “I happen to think you’re very cute.”

His heart hummed as it broke. She was into José, no doubt.

Trini squinted, worked her lips into a corkscrew smile. “Raymond, you ever meet somebody, you feel like you know them a long time? You feel like you can say anything to that person?”

“Yeah?”

“You’re like the big kid brother I always wanted.”

An asteroid the size of a cannonball dropped from high orbit and zipped through Ray’s chest at sixty thousand miles an hour. “Your big kid brother,” he said. “Cool.”

7

JOSÉ KICKED OPEN the stationhouse door, collapsed onto the couch. "Water. I'm-a die. I ain't run like that since juvie. Totally rehydrated."

"Well, we can't have y'all bein totally rehydrated. Lemme step-'n'-fetch you some water, Master."

"Please, son. I'm like to the burnin bush. Can't move. You don't *know* the hell I been through last two hours."

"Hell happened?" Ray said.

"Gimme a bottle a Polish Spring, I tell you all about it."

Ray brought the water.

José swigged, burped. "A hour and a half I'm huntin down that Richie kid. I got half our money back. Kid gonna bring me the other three dollars next week, he says, but I don't know. He got them liar eyes, the kind that . . . You listenin to me?"

"Yeah, but I can't believe what I'm hearin. You run him an hour and a half for three bucks?"

"It's the principle of the thing."

"And what's that, that we can steal but he can't?"

"Not from us." José winked. "So then I'm comin home, that punk we owe money to?"

"That Paulie cat?" Ray said.

"Mean-ass wannabe sees me countin the dough I just got off Richie, Paulie starts to chasin me. I had to run into them piles of garbage bags behind the hotel there."

"The whorehouse one on Broadway, all that stanky trash in back?"

"I'm practically rollin through it to ditch Paulie." José sniffed his armpit. "I stink like whorehouse trash now. Gimme a bar a soap, I'm goin to the river."

"Hold up a sec. I gotta talk to you about somethin."

"Hell's wrong with you? Look like you gonna cry."

"I ain't gonna *cry*. Show you how much of a crier—"

"A'right, a'right, c'mon, talk quick. The waters are callin."

"You take her, the girl. Trini."

"Trini? That girl?" José smoothed his cornrows, caught himself, stopped. "Nah, son, you saw her first. You take her."

"I can't take her. She don't want me to took her."

"Nah, Ray, man, she likes you, man. I seen it."

"Not like she likes you. She *likes* you."

"Whoa, whoa, whoa, hold up a damn minute here. Whoa."

José plunked onto the bunk next to Ray. "She *said* she likes you?"

"Phew, sit downwind, will ya? No, she said she likes *you*."

"That's what I meant. But she *said* it?"

"What, that she likes you?" Ray said.

"What are we talkin about here? Yeah, that she likes me."

"She almost said it," Ray said.

"Hell?"

"I go, 'You like José?' And she's like, 'He's okay.'"

"Holy. Shit. Serious? She said *he's okay*? Dag, son."

"Told ya," Ray said.

"Dag, this is serious." José flopped back on the bed. "What I'm opposed to do now?"

Ray spit out the window. "I want you and her to, you know."

José nudged Ray. "You gonna be sad?"

"Psh, course not." Ray smoothed what was left of his hair.

"You're *sure* about this."

"Psh, course."

José looked at the Fatty dog. "She likes me, you fat dope."

The dog looked at José out the sides of its eyes.

"He's too lazy to turn his head," José said. "Damn dog creeps me out, man."

"Leave 'im alone," Ray said. "You take the niece and I'll keep tryin to work my way in with the old lady."

"Son, you're the best man at my weddin."

"Shut up, man. You cook tonight."

José chucked his arm over Ray's shoulder. "Ray-Ray, I'm-a steal us a nice home-cooked meal."

◆

They were at Yolie's door before the joint opened. Trini re-rowed José's do while Yolie just stared at Ray's near baldy. "I dunno what you want me to cut, amor."

"Shave it."

Yolie sucked her teeth and draped her breasts over Ray as she shaved his head. Ray was as happy as a miserable man can be. He looked kind of mean bald. He liked the look. Superslick assassin. Mond, Ray Mond.

Without the chick.

That night at the new *Spider-Man* movie Trini sucked a necklace of welts onto José. The slurping sound drove Ray nuts. He said he had to go to the bathroom, never came back, hopped the train downtown to the all-night Home Depot. He liked hanging out there. They gave free classes about plumbing, wiring and how to pick rugs and drapes that created harmonic ambience.

On the train ride home he read this book that said God is dead.

Ray shut the book. "Bummer."

He came in late. José was doing Grand Theft on the big screen. Scarface cheered him on from the small. Ray plopped onto the couch next to the J-man. José looked at him. "You're mad, right?"

"You're a hickey with limbs."

"Yup, he's mad," José said.

"I'm only gonna ask you one thing. Do not ever talk smack about that chick with me."

"Hell you talkin about?"

"Like, 'Smell my fingers,' stupid shit like that."

"Number one, she ain't like that, you should know. And third of all, I ain't like that."

"You talk smack about chicks all the time!"

"S'pose you're right. But not about her. She's so cool, Ray."

"I don' wanna know."

"C'mon, man, you're m' boy. I can't tell you, who'm I gonna tell?"

"You love her, I know."

"How'd you know?"

"I'm goin a bed."

José rummaged through the Home Depot shopping bag. "Anythin to eat in here?"

"I ain't even gonna answer that." Ray kicked aside José's mountain of clothes to get to his ratty old juvie duffel, pulled out his Nets pj's. He was a Knicks fan, but Macy's only had Nets the day he and José had gone "shopping."

José was wearing Nets jammies too. Even in summer the night breeze off the river threw a damp chill over everything. José dumped the Depot bag, sorted through Ray's gets. "Hell is this for?"

"Well, it's a paint scraper, so I reckon it's for pickin teeth. Idiot."

"Raymundo Santiago, defender of New York City's mailboxes. Ray, you scratch it off, they gonna hit the box again that night. It's pointless."

"It ain't pointless."

"There's fifty million rotten things written all over Bronx mailboxes, and if I froze the world still to keep new ones from goin up, and then I gave you all the paint scrapers in the world, you'd still never get the job done. Now gimme some cigarette money."

"I hid it in the dog chow."

"Makin me fish through goddam dog food now." José pulled on his jeans, grabbed some money, headed out, held up at the door. "Hey, Ray? If you didn't want me to go out with her, then why'd you set us up, man?"

A few seconds later Ray heard José whistling "Love Me Tender" on his way uphill. He had a great whistle. Ray couldn't whistle for shit. He looked at the paint scraper. "Fuck, man." He chucked it into the garbage.

The dogs' ears went up. Out the window, in the weeds downhill, methamphetamine pipes flared. Ray grabbed his baseball bat. "Sing," he whispered to the dogs.

The dogs howled. The junkies ran. Ray slept bat in hand.

Next morning Trini brought them breakfast. She was cool in front of Ray. She mussed his scalp as much as she mussed José's cornrows. "My cousin's coming up from the island, Raymond."

"Okay?" Ray said.

"I told her about you. You wanna double-date like?"

"Okay."

"She's stayin a month, comin up in three weeks."

"Okay."

"But you're gonna have to come on up to my tía's. I don't want to bring her down here, no offense."

The boys were quiet. José shrugged. "You don't like our house?"

Trini sat in the middle of the couch, patted the spaces at her sides. "Sit."

The boys and six or so dogs climbed onto the couch. José started to shove them off but stopped. He made sure Trini saw he was petting them.

Trini looked around the stationhouse. "We got to get you boys into a real home."

"Anyplace you are, T-mamita, that's home to us," José said. "That's got to be the smoovest dag thing I ever said."

"That was pretty smooth," Trini said.

Ray wondered if the cousin looked like Trini. Even if she did, she wouldn't *be* Trini.

"Let's eat," Trini said. "Gentlemen, would you kindly set the table?"

"Yes'm," Ray said.

"Yo, Mr. Man, git your lazy bones in gear and help."

Dag, Ray thought, she's already calling him her man.

8

TRINI HOOKED RAY up with a summer job at Yolie's, eight bucks an hour cash to run errands, sweep the shop, take out trash, fix things Yolie could never get her landlord to fix. Plumbing, electric, carpentry, Ray knew it all thanks to Home Depot freebies and juvie shop class. Using his hands for something other than thieving was fun. He liked being busy. A month passed fast.

Yolie was a good businesswoman. She imported hard-to-get beauty supplies from Puerto Rico on the side, hair relaxer, do-it-yourself dye and the like from this company Enrique Hormón. Ray chuckled as he delivered Hormón to the old ladies too sick to come into the shop. *I'm bringin Henry The Hormone to the old gals.* Anyway, working for Yolie was better than working for Jerry, though the boys still were doing some of that.

Yolie would have made money if she didn't hand out so many freebies and pay-me-laters. If some kid came by selling candy for his ball team, Yolie gave him a twenty, told him to keep his candy and hit her a home run. She'd eye her stack of past due bills, shrug. *"Es la vida,"* she'd say, and wink at Ray.

Ray dug being around chicks all day. He noticed they had a habit of smelling clean most of the time. Sometimes Ray would have to stop what he was doing, take it all in, the different perfumes, Bubble Yum grape from all that snap-cracked gum, the women's voices, a treeful of birds chirping.

Even José was gigging. Yolie had him at The Palace until she caught him sucking face with Trini one too many times and sent him down the street to her friend Romeo's shop, The Slice Is Right. José dug pedaling pie. "They pay me to ride my bike, Ray-Ray. Find a better job in this fool country of ours." José was socking away his money to buy a motorcycle.

At day's end, going downhill to Ten Mile was tough for Ray. With José out on deliveries, late nights were lonely. Uphill here in the Heights life hummed 24/7.

And Trini was here.

She'd hang with José mornings, but she and Ray had the rest of the day together working in the shop. Trini was taking summer session physics to get a jump on junior year. Ray would hang with her after work, help her study, lose himself in her textbooks. "Please go back to school this fall?" she would beg.

And he would smile, look away, wonder if he should.

Yolie knew the boys had ditched school, but dropping out was common up here. She had dropped out herself. She told them, "Work hard, save your money, you be a'right."

José skid-stopped in front of The Palace, a stack of pie boxes strapped to the back of his bike. He banged on the shop window. Ray swung out and José gave him a brown-bag slice. "Extra cheese?" Ray said.

"Don't ever say I don't take care of my boy." José was off with a smack to the back of Ray's shaved head.

Ray got back to sweeping a mountain of hair.

Yolie was working the register, giving a lady her change, when two kids waiting for cuts started a slap-fight with each other. They were pals horsing around, but the way the cussing was flying, you wouldn't know that. One kid tripped, knocked over a folding chair. Yolie grabbed her heart at the racket.

"Yo," Ray said to the kids.

"What up?"

"Y'all take it outside." Six three, two sixty, shaved head. Ray was scary.

"We're gettin haircuts," the bigger one said.

"Not here you're not," Ray said. "Not until y'all learn some respectable language in the presence of a lady."

"Fuck you then," the kid said.

Ray took one step, the kids flew.

Ray turned to Yolie, her hand on her heart, her eyes calm.

"Sorry about that, ma'am," Ray said. He righted the upended chair.

"Amor, flip the sign to closed, lock the door, come upstairs. I want to talk with you."

Ray turned out the lights, went outside to pull in the chairs Yolie left out there for the old folks to rest in while they were shopping, dragging their carts and walkers and clunky Velcro-strap Frankenstein shoes up and down the avenue.

"Yo!" Ray heard behind him.

He spun to find a rock had been hurled at his face. He ducked. Over his head the rock smashed on the shop window and rained sticky yellow goo onto the back of his neck. Somebody had bulleted a rotten egg at him.

"Yo faggot!" The two kids he'd just tossed out of the shop were at the sidewalk edge. They flipped him off and ran.

Ray pulled a workman's rag from his back pocket, wiped the egg off his neck, cleaned the mess from the shop window. "Goddam kids."

Yolie collapsed exhausted into the old salon chair she'd had Ray bring to the upstairs kitchen, where after a full day of squeaky kids drooling over her *melones* she liked to sip herself a nice Brugal. Trini massaged her aunt's shoulders. The women were smiling.

Ray nodded his head respectfully as he came into the kitchen.

Yolie nodded back, appraised Ray. "I like having a big strong boy like you around. People respect you."

"Thanks, ma'am." He wondered if she smelled the rotten egg on him.

"You're a *man, me entiendes? Un hombre fuerte.*" Yolie tapped her heart with her knuckles.

"'Preciate that." Ray Mond, the *man*. Be shaving once a week soon.

"I'm thinking about expanding my business," Yolie said. "I'm gonna take Enrique wide, grow out from the Heights into Harlem and Inwood. I got *muñecas* up in The Bronx crying for el Hormón. I need someone to manage the orders and the deliveries. It's a big job. You gonna run it."

"Ma'am?"

Trini winked at Ray. She might as well have kissed him.

"It's gonna be a lot of work," Yolie said. "Long hours, but we gonna make a lot of money. You save, you buy you mami a house within five years, not vinyl, brick. On the perfume alone we be millionaires. Throw in the vitamin supplements, we own the city, the Trump got nothing on us."

"Missis Yolie, I'm just about to turn fifteen. I don't know if I can—"

"Look at me. I started when I was fifteen. You good with numbers, you a hard worker, you fix anything, you don't give up, and I trust you. I'd be crazy not to make business with you. Yes or no?"

"*Hell* yes."

"Good. Just have you mami gimme a call."

Trini stopped massaging her tía's shoulders.

"My moms?" Ray said. "Wuh-why?"

"You ain't gonna be home for dinner most nights. Weeks will pass and she won't see you. I just want to talk with her first, explain the opportunity, the sacrifice, make sure it's okay with her."

"Oh, it's okay with her, ma'am. I'm sure of it."

Behind her tía's back Trini folded her arms, gave Ray mean eyes, mouthed *Tt, Raymond!*

Yolie reached over her shoulder, took Trini's hand, gently brought Trini to her side. "Why is he lying to me, and about what?"

"I better go," Ray said.

Yolie said, "Sit down, amor. Trinita, start talking."

Trini told Yolie that Ray and José had no parents. She told her the boys were living on their own.

Yolie calmly took in the info. "And why now you're telling me this, Trinita? Why would you lie to me?"

"I *didn't* lie. You never asked. I wouldn't *lie* to you. But now that it came up—"

"Do I have to tell you with your A averages that holding back is lying, chica?"

"Tt, I, like, was afraid you wouldn't let me hang out with them," Trini said.

"Because they have no parents? Is that what you think of me? And you, señor, why you were afraid to tell me these things?"

"Sorry, ma'am."

Yolie stared at Ray for a long time, her anger turning soft, her eyes beginning to get wet.

Now that Yolie had offered him a partnership in her business Ray wanted to tell her that he was on the lam, that he had a record, but Trini would freak out. She had no idea the boys had crime in their past.

Yolie seemed to decide not to cry, winked at Ray, sipped her Brugal. "Okay. Here's what we gonna do. You amors gonna come live here with us, you and the José."

Trini mugged her tía with kisses.

"You gonna live in the attic," Yolie said. "You got your own bathroom up there. Needs work, but you fix it."

"I ain't know what to say, ma'am."

"Say yes. I like that word. First thing you gonna fix for me? Put a lock on chiquita's door."

"My door?" Trini said.

Yolie nodded at Ray. "Him I'm not so worried about, but that José is a little wolf."

Trini blushed. "He ain't like that, Tía."

"Oh, he's like that," Yolie said. "Trust me. He wouldn't be a man if he wasn't."

Then what's that make me? Ray wondered.

On the way to Ten Mile Trini chattered on about how they could fix up the attic, about how the boys would have a future now. That Enrique Hormón would make everybody rich, that the boys could go back to school, Ray to some fancy college someday. "You don't seem too excited," she said.

"Just thinkin," he said.

"About what?"

That you're about to find out José ain't comin uphill, not even for you. "Nothin."

"Raymond, what'd my tía just say? No secrets. Do you want to live with us or not?"

More than anything. "I'm just wonderin what we're gonna do with the dogs."

"They're comin, *bato*. Think I'd let 'em starve down here? We got the yard out back. Come night, put a couple in my room, couple in the attic with y'all until we adopt 'em out into good homes. I got all these friends downtown at school, they're into the pet rescue thing big time. We keep a couple pups at The Palace, everything is everything."

"You got it all worked out, huh, uptown to downtown. You ought to run for mayor."

Trini smiled, grabbed Ray's hand, "Check it: Couple days ago we're talkin about you, José says, 'I do believe Ray is smart enough to become President of the United States of North America someday.' He's so cute."

"Yeah. Cute." Ray looked at Trini's delicate hand in his monster paw.

She hooked her arm through his, back swung her foot to kick his butt. He jammed his hands into his pockets to keep from pulling her into a kiss.

They went into the stationhouse, found José shirtless, hanging upside down from a roof rafter, laughing himself to tears. "Found me a pair of gravity boots on the street! Better than drinkin beer! Yo, I am upside-down dru-*hunk*!"

"Antigravity boots," Ray mumbled.

"Git on down from there!" Trini said. "Break your fool neck."

José undid the clips holding the boots to the rafter, dropped down to the couch in a half flip, perfect ten.

"What up." He pulled in Trini for a kiss.

Trini pushed him off. "All sweaty. Yuck. Okay, hombre, pack your bags. You boys are movin into my aunt's attic."

José stopped laughing. *"What?"*

"Serious," Trini said. Now she kissed him.

José backed away from Trini's kiss, kicked off the antigravity boots, chucked them to Ray, chucked them hard. "You in on this too?"

Ray shrugged, squeezed into the sweaty boots, moped over to the ladder that went up to the roof rafter.

"Will y'all stop messin with them fool boots? Be *care*ful Raymond," She squinted at José. "What all's your problem? You wanna stay *here*? With the bugs, the damp, sleepin with ball bats every night?"

"Damn straight," José said.

"And you don't care how that makes me feel? That I worry about y'all every minute you're down here."

"Then don't worry, T," José said. "Serious, I am not goin uphill. Goddam curfews, have to quit smokin, can't drink no more, gettin yelled at, pick up your damn clothes, do this, do that, everybody callin me a stupit idiot, gettin smacked around—"

"J, it's Yolie, man," Ray said. "Yolie's cool, yo."

"I know, still . . . dag. Shit." José nodded to Ray. "You all go on up you want to, homeboy. Serious. You be better off. But me, I gotta stay put."

"José, my aunt would never hit you. The smokin and drinkin, yeah, you'll have to cut back, but—"

"No. That's my final." José made for the door.

"Don't you walk away from me, Mister Man."

"I gotta go to work." He grabbed his bike, held up. "Ray, make sure you walk her uphill. I don't like her in the woods alone." He left.

Trini spun to Ray. Even upside down she was perfect, her eyes wet, her breath fast. "Hell is *wrong* with him?"

Upside down, Ray wanted to hug her but couldn't take his arms away from his sides, or his shirt would fall down and she'd see his flab. "He ain't made for the home life."

Something banged on the far side of the stationhouse. The Fatty dog had just walked into a wall. Just as Ray suspected, the dog was going blind. The dog stared at the wall, walked into it again. Trini led the dog out. In the door frame and the late-day light her silhouette was angelic. She flipped her hand Miss Thing style. "Forget about bato boy, you're coming up, though, right?"

Ray's head ached from hanging upside down. He sighed. "Can't."

"You can, but you won't leave your boy, I know."

He reached out to her, his shirt came down, exposed his gut. A paperback fell out of his back pocket.

She picked it up. *"Introduction to Advanced Particle Physics."* She nodded, cried a little as she hurried out of the stationhouse.

"Wait, woman, lemme walk you home." Ray unclipped the boots from the rafter. In his jostling, the rafter cracked. He dead dropped, broke the couch. The fat dope dog limped in and sat on Ray's chest.

9

ON THE WAY up to Yolie's Ray ran into José speeding down the avenue with a delivery. José skid-stopped his bike, the pies went flying. "She's mad, right?"

"More hurt."

"She cry?"

"Yup."

"Shit. Help me pick up this goddam pizza."

Ray helped José scoop up the pizza that had fallen out of the boxes wet side down onto the street. They brushed the dirt off it, joggled the cheese, made the pies nice in the boxes.

José strapped the boxes to his bike. "Whachou doin out here anyways? You goin a talk to her?"

"Yup."

"I'll try to smoov things out with 'er tomorrow mornin.

But Ray? I ain't livin over that Braid Palace. She can leave me, I'm still down at Ten Mile."

"I know."

"You got gum?"

"Just ABC style."

"I'll take it," José said.

Ray spit out his gum, ripped it, gave half to José.

"Yo, somethin else," José said.

"Tell it."

"Jerry called The Slice lookin for me."

"How'd he know you're workin at The Slice?"

José shrugged. "Scary, huh? He got a sweet one goin down tonight. I told him we do it."

"Yeah, huh? I dunno."

"Ray, please, man. Dukie, I'm thirteen hundrit bucks away from gettin me my Ninja, man. Paulie gonna give it to me cut rate."

"You're talkin to him when we owe him dough?"

"Punk mugged me. Ordered a pie to his apartment, I knock on the door, next thing I know I'm on the floor. Was such a sweet move I couldn't even be mad about it. Sometimes you gotta tip your hat. Anyway, we square with 'im now. But I don't get that bread to 'im end of the week, he gonna sell the bike to somebody else."

"There's other Ninjas out there, man. You keep hustlin pie the way you doin, you have that thirteen hundred in no time at all."

"I do the Jerry, I got my bread *tonight*. Last time, Ray-Ray, I promise. I see you later. Don't be late." José sped off. "And leave that paint scraper home, Mailbox Man."

"Riskin my Enrique future for a goddam secondhand Ninja." Ray spit his gum into the trash. Friends to the ends be a heavy load sometimes.

Ray rang the door buzzer. Yolie leaned out the window over The Palace, dropped the keys to Ray. He let himself in and upstairs.

"Trinita told me about the José."

"She around, ma'am?"

"Homework at a friend's. Talk to him. Tell him to relax. I'm not a cop, okay? You know me."

"I know, ma'am. Missis Yolie, I talk with you a sec?"

"Ob'course. Come, we talk in the attic. I show you." She took his hand, led him upstairs.

Boxes of Enrique Hormón cluttered the attic. "We put this stuff down the basement, plenty of room for you two, right?"

The streetlight bled through the faded cheesecloth curtains, painted the floor soft silver. Not only did the bathroom have a shower, it had a toilet. No more squatting in the Ten Mile woods.

"Washing machine and dryer in the basement."

No more lugging laundry uphill to the Spin-'n'-Win on slippery winter days.

Ray looked out the back window, took in the yard with its bamboo and palms, a tiny aboveground pool. He'd been in the back to work but hadn't seen it from this high up, all at once. It was a patch of oasis amidst the city concrete.

"For your babies, they can sun themselves all day, you build a doggy door, they come and go in and out the house when they want. Nice, no?"

Ray nodded. "Nice."

"You pale, amor." She felt his forehead. "What's wrong?"

"Ma'am, before you bring me in on the Hormón and all, there're some things you should know about me."

"Okay?"

"I, like, got a record, ma'am. Me and José. We're on the skipped parole list."

Yolie didn't blink. "A'right, what else? Amor, don't look so surprised. You think I'm bata, hijo? Old Yolie knows what time it is. Why else would you be hiding down there in the park? I grew up here back in the day, okay? We did what we had to do to get by. I know where you from, and you welcome here, my home, my business. You special, chico. I got a feeling about you. Look at you face now. Raymundo, *coño,* don't worry so much. It's not the end of the worl, okay? It'll be a'right. C'mere, give Mami a hug." She pulled him into a tight one.

Her breasts crushed him, but he didn't want to sex her up. He didn't want to cry either, but he did.

"How could you lie to me like that?" Trini said.

Ray spun around, found Trini standing in the doorway, schoolbooks in hand.

"Y'all are criminals?" she said. "Y'all thug-hustled me."

"Trin, I'm sorry—" Ray said.

Yolie cut in, "Chica, how dare you judge him? You hold back on me, and that's okay, but he holds back on you, it's not? This boy is your friend. Now, I'm not having this in my house, this bad feelings. You two go downstairs, talk this out, make friends again. Go 'head, *vayan, hagan amigos*. I have to cook the books for tomorrow with the accountant and I don't have time for this nonsense. Go on now, make up."

Ray was embarrassed he'd cried in front of not one chick but two. He wiped his eyes on his sleeve. Trini pushed him into a salon chair, sat in the one next to him. "How could you not tell me?" She kept her voice down, but she was angry.

"Like you said before, we were afraid you wouldn't hang with us."

"What'd you do? What crimes?"

"Mostly bennies—breakin and enterin. Some grand larceny that got bumped down on a plea. We never hurt nobody."

"Right, you just stole their money."

"We stole food, mostly. At first."

"I must have *Sucker* tattooed on me somewhere I don't see. Here my heart's breakin for you boys, all those sob stories about foster care—"

"Yo." He calmed himself. "Those were true."

His anger surprised her. She looked away, pouted. "Ttt."

He studied her in the mirror's reflection, found Yolie in her eyes, the fullness of her lips. "How come your aunt ain't married?" Ray said.

"Lost her man in Gulf One, never got over it." She turned back to Ray. "This whole import business thing, she's doing it for you, you know? She doesn't give a damn about the money. She talks about you every night, says she thinks you're gonna be a big man someday, somebody gives you half a chance. She's your half a chance, and y'all are too stupid to come on uphill. What a waste."

"I'll talk to him, T. The J-man, he's set in his ways, though. Give him a little time to settle down. We'll see. I gotta tell you, though, I'm a little worried about bringin trouble to your aunt. Some neighbor gets mad at her, drops a dime, cops find out she's harborin two fugitives in her attic—"

"You know how many illegals she's hidden in that attic while they were on their way to getting green cards?"

"Harriet Tubman of Washington Heights, huh?"

"Raymond, you can't lie to me like that, not ever again, okay?"

"Okay."

"And promise me y'all aren't gonna do any more rustlin."

"No more rustlin," he said. *If I can get out of this last job tonight,* he didn't say.

10

RAY KNOCKED ON Jerry's door. José could wait another goddam month or so for his Ninja.

"Round Face. You're early." Jerry looked out into his lot. "Where's the ride?"

"Yeah, um, about that. We don't wanna do it."

Jerry frowned. "Well, you're gonna do it anyway."

"Look man, I came here out of courtesy—"

"No, you came because you know if you scooch out on me I'll have somebody ram a screwdriver through the back of your beach ball head there, and you're right. Listen, it's too late now, kid. Yous are either bringing me a Lincoln Navigator or a pair of thumbs."

"How's that?" Ray said.

"I already got a buyer gave me half the money. This is gonna be an ek-scape vehicle this thing yous're boosting tonight. I scooch this guy and the guy, he's this maniac Russian, he'll cut off my thumbs. Now, if I'm short a pair of thumbs I'll need yours for replacements, see? You and José, which one of you's a lefty?"

Ray liked his thumbs, especially when they were attached to his hands. "Okay, but this'll be our last job with you."

"Right. Yous kids, you'll be back again next week begging me for work."

"Don't bet your daughter's Catholic school tuition on it," Ray said.

"Talkin about my daughter, Round Face? Half-breed mutt. Get over to that vehicle heist before I pop a cap into your fat ass."

Ray left. "Asshole."

"Don't try to skip out on me, Ray. Wherever yous go, I'll find you. Believe me."

Ray believed him.

Some gangbanger leaned out of a bass-booming, cruising Mercedes, chucked a Dunkin' Donuts bag into the street. A flock of lean pigeons dropped down on the fresh trash.

"How'd I get here?" Ray said to the pigeons.

The pigeons didn't give a damn about Ray. They pecked that Dunkin' waste as if it were manna.

"Four hours ago I'm promisin her I'm-a go clean, here I am again, hidin in the park bushes, lookin to boost an eighty-five-thousand-dollar ride that's gonna be used as an escape vehicle for drug runners, a hit maybe? That woman's brain is an audio recorder, girl remembers what you said word for word from the day she met you. She finds about this, she's gonna play me back that conversation to the syllable, 'And then *you* said, No more rustlin, and then *I* said—'"

José skidded up, a pie box strapped to the back of his bike. "You gotta stop talkin to yourself, Ray. I seen you, son, from halfway up the block. It's gettin serious. That was a full-out conversation you were havin with you."

"I was talkin to the pigeons."

"What a relief. Fourteen skippin straight to salinity."

"Senility."

"Like I said." José broke out the pizza, slapped some into Ray's hand. "The mark park his Navvie yet?"

"Nope. *Damn* this sausage smells good."

"Only reason I work at that place, the sausage pie. I'm goddam addicted to it. Hoo, son, I am jacked up tonight. I can almost feel that Ninja throttle in my right hand. Vrrm-vrrrrooom."

"This is my last heist job, J. Serious."

"Right, right, I know, I know. Check it out. Here's our boy now, right on schedule. Them pimps keep to a clock a'right. Workin habits are admiral."

"Admirable."

"Why you keep repeatin me all the time?"

The Lincoln Navigator ate up four squares of hydrant

sidewalk. Two blingy dudes got out, yawned, stretched, made their way into a building.

"That's some high-class velour there," José said. "Rope-a-dope gold. That's us in five years."

Ray gagged on a glob of pizza cheese knotting in his throat.

José slapped Ray's head. "You don't like it, go to school come fall."

"Hell with that."

"Up to you. A'right then, let's do it, brother."

Just like last time, they jimmied the lock clean and quiet, clipped the alarm before it blipped twice. Ray slid into the driver's seat. José swung his bike into the back, took shotgun lookout.

Ray made the first stretch of road fine. The next stretch he swerved to avoid hitting a squirrel, plowed the car into a tree. The air bags popped.

"Dag, man!" Ray said. "Yo! Ah God. Sorry, man!" He was covered in airbag powder.

José wiped the powder from his face. "All to spare a squirrel. Gonna catch that critter, make you eat it raw."

Ray hyperventilated.

"Easy, kid. You're a'right." José pulled his airbag clear of his body, laughed. "All this powder, ain't gonna be too hard to spot us. We be like Casper without the cash."

Ray tried to pop his seat belt, jammed locked. "Git, J! Run, man!"

"The hell I will." José wrestled Ray's seat belt, no go.

The sirens came fast.

"J, *please,* man. Yo, I'm beggin you, just leave me, man."

"Scarface don't leave his pals behind."

"Hell with Scarface, yo. This is real time now."

"Ain't I know it."

The spared squirrel settled on a branch overhanging the crashed car, chucked an acorn hull onto the car hood as it stared at the boys.

Ray punched the dashboard. "José, man, just leave me *alone,* man."

The Five Two was jamming with criminals, a line of perps and their catchers snaking all the way up to the booking desk.

"How long you reckon we get?" Ray said.

"Year, prob'ly. Year ain't bad." José winked. "Out in six on good b."

"Yup," Ray said.

The desk sergeant was tired but almost nice. "You want to call anybody? You *got* anybody to call?"

They weren't talking, only to each other. Ray mouthed to José, *Yolie?*

José shook no.

"Fellas, I'm gonna find out your names sooner or later." The sergeant called for a cop to take the boys back to a holding cell.

On the way down the hall José whispered, "We prob'ly don't want Trini knowin about this one. She kill us, she finds out we swiped a car. She don't even like me playin Grand Theft on the *Tee*Vee."

"Gonna hurt her bad, not knowin where we went."

"I'll let her know at some point," José said. "Meantime, nothin to be done about it, her wonderin. Hurts me more than her, her sadness, but that's just the way it is."

"Yo, José, man!" some kid called from behind the cell bars.

"Yo, Tivo, what up, kid!" José threw a nod and a grin Tivo's way.

Tivo was in a tagger crew Ray and José had run with in juvie. They called him Tivo because he did great impressions. "Yo y'all, look yo, it's the J-man, yo!" He busted out his José impression, slick movie star style. "'Yo, *kid,* what up, *son*? Where's the shorties at, *bro*thuh?'"

The crew had been booked all together. They brightened at seeing José. "Yo, José man, what up?"

"'Sup, José?"

"Yo, remember me, J-man?"

He's rolling in welcome as Jesus on the palms, Ray thought. He wished he had that in him, that king thing. He nodded hi to the fellas in José's wake, but nobody noticed him.

The cop put them into a holding cell.

"God damn you, man," Ray said. "How you so mad cool all the time? You ain't worried a *lick,* are ya?"

"Why worry?" José smiled. "We be a'right, Ray-Ray. You see."

No sooner had the door shut than another cop, the arresting officer, came back. "Now I know who you two are. You were the ones that broke into that supermarket on Broadway a couple years back, right? The Bread Thieves, we were calling you. You break into a store full of cash registers, and all you take is ten loaves of Wonder."

Ray was embarrassed.

José grinned. "That's us, the Wonder Thieves."

"Yeah well, you two been running together too long. Have the whole house throwing a riot inside of a day. I'm splitting you up." The cop nodded to Ray. "You, Big Boy, let's go."

Ray cuffed, José cuffed, their hands behind their backs, they went back to back, grabbed hands. "Peace, yo," Ray said over his shoulder.

José squeezed Ray's hands, whispered over his shoulder, "Be cool, kid. Be brave, Ray. I see you. I see you, brother."

"All right, break it up," the cop said. He led Ray away.

"Ain't nothin but a thang, Ray," José called through the bars. "We be a'right, kid. I see you in six. We be a'right."

"Yup," Ray said, except the word died in his throat. He looked back once, over his shoulder.

Head down, José was resting his head against the bars, shaking his head. He was crying.

◆

After Ray pled down he was locked up in The Sprungs, where he would sit for a week or more while awaiting sentencing. The Sprungs was a juvenile detention unit on Rikers Island just east of The South Bronx, two hard shell tents in the airport's takeoff path, three hundred yards across the water in Queens. Every thirty seconds, *Boom!. . . Boom!. . . Boom!* the tent plastic rattled. No cells here, just six hundred rickety cots, a scratchy blanket per kid. Yelling that never stopped, piss puddles, snickering.

The snickering as Ray walked in.

They had put Ray in with the big kids this time.

The biggest kid stepped to Ray. "Whassup *mariposa*?"

With one throw, the game was on and then over.

Ray stared at the kid convulsing at his feet, blood trickling from his face. He stared at his hand. *My* hand did that? He'd been in fights, been tagged, but he'd never hit anyone before, not like this.

"You broke my nose." The kid spit teeth, wept. "Ah, my neck. My neck hurts. He opened up my face. I feel it. He ripped it."

Ray gulped. "I'm . . . I. Sorry."

"What?"

The other kids closed in on Ray. The guards got into it and broke everybody up. As the guards pulled him away it occurred to him that he'd put on four inches and almost a hundred pounds since his last juvie run. He was top dog now, top target.

11

SAME CRIME, SAME time. They got six months, but at different juvies. José pulled Crossroads in Brooklyn, Ray Spofford/Bridges, South Bronx. They could have walked if they served up Jerry, but they didn't. A man didn't rat.

The view out Ray's cell window was empty tarmac and the back of the kitchen, Dumpsters full of food, party central for the rats who seemed to say, *No,* you *move,* when they crossed paths with the kitchen workers. Days became weeks, each hour an eon, the heat shimmered less off the tarmac, dead leaves from weed trees scraped across the lot. Then the snow fell, and the tarmac was for the shortest time pink crystals before it turned to slush. Then the last day came.

Ray gathered his few things, thought about this last juvie run, what he'd learned after all the hours of feeling like an idiot because he couldn't muster the guts to run over a squirrel. The gray hours of lame school, group counseling, kids falling asleep, sliding out of plastic chairs. He'd learned something, all right: Yet again, he'd learned nothing.

He'd relearned a couple of things, though: Outside was better than inside. That he had been caught being desperate and stupid, he'd be desperate and stupid again, he'd be caught again, if he wasn't killed first.

He packed his brown paper bag with books, his underwear—he had nothing else. A local prep school had donated the out-of-date science texts, better than nothing and much better than the prison library, *See Spot Run*. He studied his hands, bigger, harder than when he'd come in six months before, his knuckles scarred from that first day when he cracked that kid's teeth. He'd been jumped a few times after that, crushed his attackers until no one jumped him anymore and the fellas let him keep to himself. The realization hit him only now: He was a tough kid. Maybe even a man. Un hombre fuerte.

He eyed his sill and the last thing left to pack, a stack of letters. He'd written to Yolie his first day in, to apologize. He'd written to Trini every day after. He'd never sent any of the letters. He flushed the letter to Yolie down the toilet, and then the rest of the stack, a love letter a flush.

"Afraid to mail a letter. Un hombre fuerte. Sure."

◆

"Now, Raymundo," the parole officer said, "you know the drill here."

"I do. Yes, ma'am. I know it."

"This couple that's taking you in, they're very strict."

"I understand." Ray jiggled his foot to reposition the tracking device bracelet choking his ankle.

"Raymundo, do you promise to—"

"To be a good boy, you bet, I promise. I double swear it I will."

The P.O. nodded, shook her head, nodded, shook and stamped Ray's papers.

The foster parents drove Ray north to Bronxville, what the J-man would call a white folks' town. Jesus on the cross hung from the BMW's rearview. Out the window the snow was deep. The old man gave Ray a lecture, Ray cried in all the right spots, swore up and down he'd be a good boy, had the guy and his old lady bawling. They told him he was going to Fieldston, a swanky prep school. He'd placed into the gifted and talented group because of his PSATs, which they made him take at juvie. He pretended to be thrilled. He ripped open his jacket and mopped his brow with his shirt.

"Want me to turn down the heat, Raymundo?" The old lady said his name as if it were three words.

"I'm fine, ma'am."

"I really wish you'd call me Mom," she said.

What the hell. "Thank you, Mom." Ray sniffled and kissed her hand, and she cried so hard Ray thought she would bust her eyes.

As they drove through the town Ray looked for some grime and the comfort it might have given him, but even the curb snow was white. The people looked as if they had stepped out from catalog pages, bright new clothes, perfect hair. Ray rolled down the window and spit.

"Please don't do that, Ray Moon Do."

"Yes, *Mom*. Sorry."

"Easy, Elaine," the old man said.

"It's a violation. They fine people for that kind of behavior."

The old man winked at Ray from the rearview. "One step at a time, right, kiddo?"

"Yup," Ray said. "Real sorry about that."

"How you feeling, Sport?"

Sport said, "Real, real good, *Dad*."

A sad maid served dinner. Ray helped her with the dishes. He tried to talk with her, gave her a go in English then in Spanish, got nothing.

He looked around the house for signs of a dog, but there were no dogs. The house smelled like flowers, but there weren't any flowers. On top of the toilet Ray found flower spray. He came back out to the table for dessert. "Ray Moon Do," Dad said. "Was thinking we could jog on down to the model store tomorrow, grab ourselves a sailboat or two."

"Oh, you'll have a fine time, Ray Moon Do. There's a miniature train that rides around the store!"

"*Awe*some!"

The old folks showed him to his posh room, big as the Ten Mile River stationhouse, tucked him to bed. The old lady kissed his forehead. Her lips were dry. For half a minute Ray thought about riding out the next six months here until he turned sixteen, when he could declare himself an emancipated minor. He could hook up with Yolie and Trini and do the Enrique Hormón thing. "Nah, you fucked that one up beyond fixing. They'll hate you into the next life."

Ray waited until he heard his foster parents go to bed, their voices muffled through the wall, their whispers hopeful. He heard *good boy* over and over. Half an hour later he snuck downstairs, found the old man's wallet and cigarettes, grabbed a book from the library and slipped out a basement window.

An hour later he was at the train station. As he waited for the southbound he read the book he'd swiped from the old man's den. Some Buddhist cat assured Ray that life was meaningless. This was supposed to make Ray feel free. It didn't. It made him feel meaningless.

The train let him off in The West Bronx, a ten-minute walk from Jerry's Auto Glass. Ray popped the lock and waited.

Jerry showed early—Jerry was an early riser, you had to give him that much. He didn't like finding Ray in his office. "Round Face, huh?"

"See you still got your thumbs there, Jerry."

"Lucky me. Get outta my chair."

Ray got up.

"So yous kept quiet, huh?" Jerry wiped his nose on his sleeve. "Not that it matters. Cops got nothing on me but parking tickets."

"I need a favor."

Jerry squinted. "Okay?"

Ray rolled up his pant leg. "Cut it off."

Jerry took Ray into the shop, grabbed his three-foot clippers, cracked the titanium tracking bracelet strangling Ray's ankle. Ray bounced.

"Wait."

"What."

Jerry stuffed two grand into Ray's hand, Ray dropped it, kept going.

"Don't be like that, kid, c'mon. 'Ey, come next week. Maybe I got something for you."

"Not interested."

"Something legit, I mean."

Ray kept walking. He checked Dad's wallet. Three hundred eighty bucks. He should have taken Jerry's money. "Genius." He walked to the zoo, waited for it to open, chucked the ankle bracelet into the lions' feeding cage.

He went to a diner to get warm, stuffed himself with pancakes, fries, Coke, fell asleep at the back table. The diner was a dive, empty, and the waitress let him sleep.

Sometime later he felt a hand on his shoulder, jumped, the waitress's hand on the back of his neck. "The hell?" He jerked away from the waitress. "Where am I?"

"El Fogonero."

"El—the firefighter?"

"The diner. That's its name. You shaking. You was talking in you sleep."

The table was wet from where Ray had rested his head to sleep. He wiped the drool from the table with his sleeve, wiped his mouth.

"You was crying," the waitress said.

"I, damn. Sorry."

"Baby, lemme make you a hot chocolate, bring you some pie. On me."

"Thank you, ma'am." Ray looked out the window. The bank clock said afternoon. "But I gotta go." The waitress went to get the bill. Ray left a hundred-dollar tip under his dirty plate.

12

WINTER COVERED TEN Mile River in three feet of icy snow. Ray followed the sneaker tracks to the stationhouse, saw the TV flicker, smiled. *"Scarface."* His smile faded. Turn around. Run.

But then that old feeling came back, a vague memory of the J-man howling.

That laugh.

Ray kicked in the door, dropped his knapsack, pulled a boxer's pose. "'Sup."

José bounced off the couch. "'Sup." He punched Ray. "How was yours?"

Ray punched back. "It was nothin. Yours?"

"Nothin. Ray-Ray. The double Ray. Dag, son, *'sup*?"

"'Sup. Dag, you took off a coupla pounds, huh?"

"Prison food. You put on a few. My boy's huge!"

"Prison food. Place is trashed, huh?"

"And here I thought I done a good job cleanin up," José said.

"Pipe heads?"

"They was too stoned to steal the *Tee*Vee. Knocked it over, got lines in it now."

"When you get free?"

"Two days back. Kid Ray, back in business!" José jumped Ray.

Ray body slammed José to the couch broken from Ray's fall from the ceiling rafter seven months before. "Where's the dogs?"

"Whores. They'll be back soon as they smell us cook somethin."

"You been back two days and you ain't cooked?"

"Cereal. The Capitán. Don't look at me like that. I was waitin for you to cook me somethin."

"That sure I'd be back, huh?"

"Where else you gonna go?"

Ray faked a grin.

"Where'd you dump your bracelet?" José said.

"Lions. You?"

"Smokestack. Yo, c'mere. I gotta show you somethin. Ray, wait'll you see 'em."

"Them?"

José led Ray down to the unheated basement, where two blue bodies hugged.

"God. Damn," Ray said. "Jesus. Pipe heads you think?"

"Shooters, tracks on their arms. Suicide pact, I make it."

Ray toed the frozen bodies, afraid they might jump up. A man and a woman dead in each other's arms. It was the saddest, filthiest, most beautiful thing he'd ever seen. "How'd you get 'em down here?"

"They was down here already." José grabbed the man's frozen leg and slid him, the two bodies frozen solid, frozen together. Under the man's leg was a shot-out hypodermic needle. The bodies were skinny, young.

"You been up there two days watching TV, and all the while they were down here?"

"They dead, son," José said. "What they gonna do to me? It's the livin folks I worry about. What oughta we do with 'em?"

"We gotta get 'em outta here. Spring comes, they thaw, rats'll come."

"And we got enough pests around here with the roaches, the damn dogs when they come back." José warmed his hands with his breath. "Let's bag 'em and drag 'em."

"Like, put 'em in the regular old garbage?"

"No, in the special garbage. The hell they feed you in that Spofford?"

"Ain't right," Ray said.

"That's about the stupidest thing I ever heard."

"Leavin Earth like they done, I gotta give 'em a proper funeral."

"That right there is what too much readin gets you, 'Leavin Earth.' Son, you don't *gotta* do it. Plus, you got eyes? The river's froze."

"Not all the way out. In the middle it's open, dammit."

"You're jokin, right? He's not jokin. Ray, we get caught draggin human Popsicles onto the river ice, folks are gonna start askin us a thing or two!"

"We can tarp 'em in the rowboat with the army tent, they'll look like bunched sail, we sled 'em down."

José rolled his eyes. "Gonna be dark soon, moron. Barge'll run us down in the black. Then you got the icebreakers. I don't know about you, kid."

"I don't know about me either."

"Punk does six and some months hard time, comes out more a kid than before. A'right then, let's chuck these lovers into the river before the goddam sun sets."

They covered the bodies with a heavy tarp, pushed their stolen rowboat through the snowy woods to the overpass. Snow fell hard, the wind picking up. A crow swung with the branch it sat. Ten Mile River was empty.

"Snow'll make for a pretty funeral," Ray said.

"'Pretty funeral.' Idiot. Snow's our cover. Help me push this mess."

They lugged the boat up the overpass steps. "You wrote her?" Ray said.

"I'm gonna write her to tell her I'm in jail?"

"But you kissed her. You can't swap spit with a chick and then just up and disappear. When you find out you're gonna be gone for a long time, you got to write her to tell her you'll be back someday."

"You don't gotta tell me what I gotta do, Ray." José spit. "Besides, my writin is lame. I was embarrassed of her seein I can't spell good."

"I'm-a school you, startin tomorrow."

"You'll school me nothin. Hey?"

"What?"

"*You* write her?"

"Psh, I'd go behind m' boy's back like that? Psh, insultin me, man."

"You do what you want. Y'all were friends, I don't mind you writin her."

"Anyway, she ain't the type to call you out on bad spellin. They ain't like us, chicks. They got feelings."

"Talkin about chicks like he knows a damn thing about 'em."

They stopped to catch their breath.

"We oughta go see her," Ray said.

"I been thinkin about it, believe me, about her, don't think I ain't. Thinkin about you, me, her and her cousin and all, how we was opposed to go on that double date."

"Cousin's long gone by now I bet." Ray stared at the tarp over the stiffs, remembered their threaded fingers, their legs locked at the hips. He put himself in place of the dead guy and Trini in place of the dead girl, their lips near touching, their eyes at each other, leaving Earth together.

"Wake up," José said.

They set the boat at the head of the down stairway. The clouds rippled like God's shabby sheet strung out to dry, the day dying, the snow, the boat, the boys' faces cast dark blue. "Aw hell, duck." José pulled Ray below the eye line of a snowdrift.

A garbage truck banged up the Drive, kept going.

"Phew," Ray said.

"Too cold for 'phew' today. Goddam thirty degrees out here."

"You'd prob'ly still find a way to take off your shirt."

"What's this now?"

"Nothin."

They flanked the boat like bobsledders, gave it a running push, jumped in. Ray hunkered in the bow but José rode the bodies as the boat bombed the overpass steps downhill over the flatlands, skipped the breakwater onto the frozen river. The boys pushed from there. A half mile out the icebreakers had gashed the Hudson with a stripe of black water a quarter mile wide. The water was empty with the snowstorm, even the tugs lying low.

"Gettin dark fast," José said. "Let's do this."

Ray nodded at a buoy locked slantways in the ice traps. "In case the wind blows the skiff while we're doin the funeral, you wanna moor it to that buoy there so it don't blow off the ice?"

"Moor it?" José said. "Nah, grab that rope thing there and tie it to that post thing there on the bell light thing there, in case the wind blows it."

"That's what mooring it means."

"Then *moor* it," José said.

"And the boat rope's called a hawser. The post is a bollard. The—"

"Ray? I ain't out here for a vocabliary lesson, dig? You say bollard or hawser one more time and I'll leave your learned butt out here on the ice, you can sink the blue people your damn self, I swear it."

They pushed the boat to the buoy, rocked it to spill the frozen bodies onto the ice. José bunched the tarp, tucked it under the rowboat's bench seat. "*Haw*ser. Like rope ain't a good enough goddam word."

Ray tied the boat to the buoy and rang the buoy bell.

"Quit messin with that bell, ya goddam bollard. Ringin it to tell the Coast Guard we got two dead folks out on the ice. I can barely see you through the snow. C'mon, Ray, let's git this done. I wanna dump these stiffs and go apologize to my shorty, see if she'll let me put my hand up her shirt."

Ray looked away.

"Aw hell. Dag. Sorry, Ray."

Ray rang the buoy bell again, just once. "That hole right there that the hawser's goin through on the boat?"

José squinted. "You're about to work my last nerve, ain't you?"

"That's a chock."

José smacked the back of Ray's head. "Grab the blue feller's foot there and let's drag this mess to the water."

The sunset split the clouds and lit the river red for a second before it died. The wind gusted, smelled like the water, sweet funk and salt. "Little warmer out here, huh?" Ray walked right to the edge of the freeze.

"When'd you get so balls out all of a sudden?" José said. "Can't look a girl in the eyes but now he's darin death on the ice."

"Hell, I forgot to bring weights to tie round the blue folks' ankles. Now they're gonna float."

"Nah," José said. "They're heavy as hell. They'll sink sure enough."

"They're frozen, right? Look at all the ice on the river. Ice floats, man."

"Well then float they will. I ain't goin back for cinder-block now."

"Next time we gotta remember to bring brick."

"Next time, huh? Ray, ain't no next time. This is the last river funeral I'm comin to anyways. This is creepy as hell, drownin these dead folks here. Let's go. Let's dump 'em."

"Wait," Ray said. "Should we say somethin, like a prayer or some damn thing?"

"You know any goddam prayers? Aw hell. You cryin now, son?"

"Hell no," Ray said. "I got a cold comin."

"You don't even know these folks."

"It's like this ain't real. Like there's not one real thing left, know what I'm sayin?"

"No, Ray, I don't know what you're sayin. Fuck it all, will ya look at him now?" José sighed, chucked his arm over Ray's shoulder. "Ray, look here. In half a hour we're gonna be watchin the fights on HBO, droppin beers and smokin full-strength Marlboros, okay? Reds. We'll get a pizza each. Now suck it up. C'mon now, bud, it's gettin dark. Let's push 'em in."

They pushed the bodies off the ice into the river. The bodies plopped, sank, came up stuck together. The tide took them fast north.

"Sad, huh?"

"You kill me, son. You'll be my death. Sad, he says. Like a damn girl. Go untie the boat. I gotta piss."

His fingers numb, Ray had a hard time digging out the knot.

"You're cookin me a good dinner tonight for this one, bitch. You owe me big, gettin me out here. And you're cleanin the damn dishes too—daggit, look at this mess now." The wind switched, blew José's pee back at him. He spun west to pee with the wind. "*You're* sad is what's sad."

Ray popped the slipknot. The wind grabbed the boat,

blew it toward the open water. "I got it." Ray ran after the boat.

"Leave it, son," José said. "We'll steal another one. Yo, Ray, let it go!"

Ray dove to the ice, grabbed the hawser line just as the boat was about to hit the water. "Lemme ask you somethin, J."

"Answer's no."

Ray stood up, dusted the ice off his pants, took a step over what looked like a healed crack in the ice and said, "If there's no heaven, you think there's a—" as he fell through the ice.

13

THE WATER WAS black.

The tide slurped Ray out into open river so cold it burned. A slick animal grabbed his legs. Eel?

The blue folks.

"Ah!" Ray screamed underwater, regretting the scream for the air it had cost him.

Not the blue folks. José. He pulled Ray upward.

The J-man yelled underwater, then above water as he and Ray broke the surface, "—on't let go of that thing!"

"What thing!"

"The *hawser,* man! In your hand! Gimme that."

Ray had been holding the towrope the whole time. He and José reeled in the boat.

"How we get up and into it now?" José's teeth chattered.

Ray's teeth too. "Here's how we gotta do it—ah! Cold!"

"How? How we d-do it?"

"You one side, me th'other. Pull up the same time. So's we don't—"

"So's we don't tip it," José said. "Ah! Daaag! Hoooo chu-hilly!"

"You laughin?"

The tide pulled them fast into the middle of the river. José swung around to the other side of the rowboat. "Ready? One, two, three."

They kicked up and pulled. José grabbed the seat bench and humped himself into the boat. Ray, much heavier, pulled his side down into the water. José leaned back to balance the boat as he grabbed at Ray. Ray swung up into the boat, but the boat had taken on water, three inches by the time it sloshed and spread over the boat's floor.

Ray didn't know what was worse, being in the river or on it. The wind sizzled him in his wet clothes. He puked what was left of the morning's pancakes into the river. José chucked up Cap'n Crunch.

"Where's the oars?" Ray said between coughs.

"I left 'em back in the shed. Don't look at me like that. I didn't think we was gonna put the boat in the water, Ray."

"Sure, why would a *boat* go in *water* of all things?"

"In Febriary, asshole?"

Ray paddled with his hands, but the water was too cold. "Burns!"

"Get your fool hands out the water. We're the tide's boys now. Freezin to death out on the river. That's just lame with no glory to it."

Ray punched the gunnels. "Why'd you have to jump in?"

"Scarface don't play, baby. The Scar gets his friends to where they got to go, word up."

"Hate you, man."

"Yeah, and I'm thrilled with you."

"Yo, I just rode a half year a juvie 'cause you just had to get a goddam used Ninja!"

"I didn't tell you to drive into a tree! Raymundo of Ten Mile River, patron saint a the fuckin squirrels."

Ray swung at José, José ducked, swung back. The boat rocked, the boys stilled and stared at each other. Ray laughed and cried.

José just laughed. "Help me roll out the tarp."

They rolled out the tarp, used it to bail the water, doubled the tarp, huddled under it back to back, shuddering. José took off his jacket, then his shirt.

Ray howled.

"Go 'head and fun me, but you oughta do the same. Get some a that water off you." José wrung out his shirt over the side.

"My blubber-a keep me warm. Good day to be a fat boy."

"All them extra cheese slices finally paid off, huh?" José

chattered as he put on his shirt. "Wind's west. We'll make Jersey before long. I never been to a foreign state before."

They were in the wide water now, the tide fast north.

The bottom of the boat was icy, but their tarp cover trapped warm air around them as their bodies shivered to make heat.

"Smells like juvie under here, huh?" José said.

"Puke if I could."

"Tell me words. Like bollard and hawser and stuff."

"Too cold. I forget all the words to everything."

"I don't wanna know any more fancy words anyhow. I'm about to fall asleep, you believe it?"

"Me too. Maybe we're freezin to death."

"Maybe we're just exhausted because some jackass got us swimmin in the winter river." José yawned.

The tide yanked the rowboat north up the Hudson toward the George Washington Bridge.

Ray couldn't keep his eyes open. He shivered himself into what he hoped was the last sleep.

He hadn't closed his eyes more than fifteen minutes when a moan woke him, then a gasp. He jumped to a sit.

"It's the ice," José said. "It's breakin up."

"How come you didn't wake me?" Ray said.

"I tried but you batted away my hand."

All across the Jersey side the icepack had splintered. The icebreakers had opened up lines to the George Washington's towers. Ice plates stacked atop one another chaotically like debris from a demolished building.

"You hear them rumbles and clicks?" José said. "It's the devil's bowling alley down there."

A slo-mo shockwave rolled under the ice, a pump of tide.

"We're goin south now," José said.

"We gotta get off the river. Boat here's flimsy fiberglass. We cut the bottom of it on a jag of ice, we're the blue folks."

"Ray, you mention them folks again I'll chuck you overboard, the three of y'all can *leave Earth* together, knock yourselves out. I already saved your lame ass once today. Double wrap your arm in tarp. We're close enough to paddle now."

They paddled toward the Jersey shore some fifty yards off. Past that were thick woods and a few mansions. "Swank, huh?" Ray huffed.

"Swank or not this is our stop. See that huge house uphill there? Folks'll help us if we cry right."

"I'm cried out."

"*Now* he can't cry. Dag, son. You just about kill me."

They rode the tide and wind on a southwest cut to a yacht club dock.

"Mind the river mud now," José said. "Suck our feet right down into the bed, we'll never get out."

They jumped from the boat to a concrete ramp used to

trailer boats in and out of the water. They misjudged the ramp's slope in the dark, jumped in a little too early. The water was up to their waists. They muffled their screams, hissed curses instead on the odd chance any security guard happened to be down by the river smoking a blunt. They didn't need to worry. There was nothing to guard this off-season night, the yachts in dry dock.

"*Leave* the rowboat," José said.

Ray let the boat drift but snatched the tarp.

On the dock, they shook and stamped like dogs after a bath. Their pants, which had started to dry a bit in the heat under the tarp, were soaked.

José bent over and grabbed his guts.

"The hell?" Ray said.

"Your hair." José fell to his knees, screaming laughter. "You look like Don King! Your do got all bunched on top your head there under the tarp! Standin off your head like you got your finger in the toaster! Look at that nappy juvie pile, frozen rusty Brillo."

Ray tried to smooth his frozen hair, pointed to José's head. "Your cornrow tails froze. You're the Dominican Statue of Liberty."

"Don King's bastard son. The one who ain't gonna inherit!"

"Hell we laughin about? We're about to die out here."

"I know it."

They laughed until they forgot they were on a dock

at the edge of dark woods in a foreign town, freezing to death. The snow clouds ran away east, leaving behind wide western sky.

"Hoo." José laughed himself quiet.

On the other side of the woods were manor grounds and uphill the mansion they spotted from the water. "Looks like a liberry," José said.

"Like you been to the library ever."

"I seen 'em from the outside." José slapped Ray's back. "Let's check it out, partner."

The tarp wrapped around them, they worked their way uphill over the frozen snow to a back patio and a greenhouse connected to the mansion. The flower beds were bare. José tried the greenhouse door, locked. "You go right, I'll go left," José said.

They both went right.

"Oh," José said, spun off left.

Ray went around to the right side of the greenhouse and found two Dobermans staring him down.

14

THE DOBERMANS CAME on a run out of their greenhouse doggy door, tackled Ray with kisses. They were old, flabby, toothless. One rolled for Ray to pet its belly, the other ran around the side of the house. A few seconds later Ray heard a scream, a clang, a yelp and then breaking glass, all muted in the heavy wind. Ray and the other dog ran around the side of the greenhouse, found the first dog quivering in the patio snow, a blood halo black in the moonlight. Wrought iron patio chair legs stuck out from a smashed greenhouse window. José held another chair over his head, saw the second dog, wound up to club it.

Ray tackled José before the J-man could swing the chair. "Hell you doin?"

"Get offa me, Ray! Dog's gonna kill us!"

"They're nice, man! Yo, stop! They're old! They're submissive!"

"Damn dog bum-rushed me!"

"To lick ya!"

The second dog came up to the boys, licked Ray, whimpered, ran back to its brother convulsing in the snow.

"Dag! Dag." Ray checked the dying dog. "Goddammit now."

"How was I opposed to know! Git out the way, lemme put it out of its misery."

"You will not."

José pushed past Ray, clubbed the dog with the chair, killed it.

The second dog hid behind Ray, shivered. "J-man, you're evil."

"He was a goner, man. He was suf—"

The greenhouse phone rang.

"Ah hell," José said. "Silent alarm."

José, Ray, and the dog, all shivering, ran through the broken window into a greenhouse just warm enough to keep the water pipes from freezing, in the far corner two ratty dog beds, empty food bowls, soiled newspapers. The place reeked of dog waste. The boys searched the dark greenhouse for the phone.

"Check it," José said, "sticker on the window got a bell and a ear with a slashed circle over it so even retards like me can figure it out. Alarm stickers for thieves with disabilities now. Here we go." He nodded to a small wall-mounted box next to the door, snapped his fingers for Ray to check out the box. "Ray-Ray, just like a bennie, yo. Now where's the damn phone?"

In the boys' experience homeowners stuck security code stickers on the alarm boxes in case they forgot their numbers under pressure. Ray leaned on the wall to steady himself as he searched for the code, his legs dead man loaners. He found the code sticker on the bottom of the box.

José found the phone hanging from the back wall of the greenhouse, picked up. "'Lo? Thank you, yes. Yup, false alarm. *Yes.* Yeah, I'm standing by."

The phone was old school, the cord knotted like a chromosome during mitosis. Ray knew if he even mumbled the word *mitosis,* José would smack him.

José mouthed to Ray, *Gimme the code.*

Ray forced his frozen fingers to make the code numbers: flipped José off for number one, then two, three, four.

José rolled his eyes. "Code number one two three four. Yup. Yup. Yup. All good. Right, we're real happy for your business too. Uh-huh, you too." José hung up the phone.

"Poor dog's all freaked out," Ray said.

"*I'm* all freaked out. We gotta get outta these wet pants and boots, son. I can't feel my feet." José dialed 1234 on the keypad next to the back door.

They rushed the warm kitchen, ripped off their damp clothes to their drawers, except Ray kept his T-shirt on.

"Get that shirt off, Ray."

"Worry about yourself, man. Lemme catch my dag breath."

The dog bounced into the kitchen from the greenhouse, its empty water bowl in its mouth, dropped the bowl at Ray's feet. "Who'd leave dogs like this?" Ray said.

"I'm gonna find the shower," José said.

"Careful. Maybe somebody's upstairs."

"Have you left Earth, son? Nobody picked up the phone, not to mention I threw a chair through a hothouse window. I think they woulda let us know they were here by now."

Ray got the dog water, found a garbage can half full of moldy dog food in the pantry. He hit the fridge, fed the starving dog cold cuts. "Hell's goin on here? No food or water, no heat, no company. Surviving on snow-melt, huh? You're a tough old boy. How long you been alone?"

José quick-limped into the kitchen. "Who you talkin to?"

"The dog."

"Why'd I ask? I got two mad hot showers runnin upstairs. Get your fat butt up there before you die of cold." José ran upstairs, Ray ran after him. "Yours is over there." José pointed right, peeled off left.

"Thank you, God," Ray said as he sank into the steam and bled the cold from his bones.

◆

Ray slipped into a ski suit he'd found in a closet. The ski hat was definitely the old lady's—pink and yellow stripes—but it was fluffy and soft and felt nice on his forehead. He hit the kitchen, the dog at his feet. The dog hadn't left his side. "Yo, yo, I smell the J-man's cookin!"

"Yo, baby! I got a feast goin here." José had a cigar in his mouth, a flapjack flipper in one fist, cognac in the other. He brushed cigar ash off his lapel. He wore the old man's robe, a silky number printed out in leopard.

"Nice robe," Ray said.

"Nice ski suit, woman. Want a cee-gar? Guy's got a whole humidifier full of 'em."

"Humidor."

"Exactly." José fired up another Cuban, blew a perfect smoke ring, gave the cigar to Ray, who couldn't blow smoke rings worth a damn. "I cranked up the heat," José said.

"I feel it. I'm wonderin if we should mosey."

"We're good," José said. "I seen it on the calendar over the counter there. Says France clear to Monday. Double-check my dyslexic ass, you want."

"You spell good enough to get *France* right." A haze of frying butter smoked up the kitchen. "Hell you makin here?"

"Flapjacks of course. They got a Deepfreeze full of pre-made in there. I chucked some Crunch in 'em for sweetness."

"The Cap'n lives here?"

"White folks ain't stupid. Plus I'll sink some booze in 'em too, unless you got any objectives?"

Ray smiled. "No objectives here."

"Attaboy." José poured cognac into the pancakes. "I'm curious what they gonna taste like, these boozy Cap'n flap-jacks here."

"They got syrup?"

"They got every damn thing. Hey, how y'all feelin?" José said.

"Me?"

"No, the other loser behind you."

Ray looked over his shoulder. No one was there. "Good."

"Liar."

"Think I sprained my wrist when I threw my fit there back in the boat."

"Punches the boat, he does. Like it's the boat's fault."

Ray rolled his wrist. "It hurts a little when I do that."

"Then don't do that." José chugged the cognac. "Wanna go shoot some pool?"

"Nah. Okay. Maybe in a little."

"Sure," José said. "They got foosball too, if that suits you any better."

"Foosball's lame."

"You're lame."

"They got a good library down the hall there," Ray said.

"Psh."

"Yo," Ray said. "Thanks for savin my wretched lame-ass life."

"Say thanks again and I'll kill you. Anyway, I did it to spite you."

"Yeah, huh?"

"Son, dyin's easy. It's the livin that worries me. Gonna let you drown, leave me to face the craziness on my own?" José winked. "First batch of flaps looks about done."

"I'll finish cookin."

"You will so," José said. "Maybe we oughta eat that poor summabitch Dobie out back there too, so's not to waste him. A side of meat for the pancakes. Look at the way he's lookin at me. Dag, son, I'm just foolin. Think I'd eat a dog?"

"You ate raccoon before. What we gonna do with that poor dead dog?"

"Triple-bag it, pitch it in the garbage."

"The garbage? The regular old garbage?"

José threatened Ray with his flapjack flipper. "Son, you'd best shut the fuck up about the regular old garbage. I'm serious as gunfire. Stomp you like the redheaded stepson. C'mon, let's eat. We got a lot of work to do before we split. There's julery and such to be stole, praise Jesus."

Ray cleaned the kitchen spotless. Leaving somebody's house a sty after jacking it was low-class. He left a list of what they took so the people wouldn't wonder what was missing.

The boys jammed their plunder into a Mercedes, the oldest of the four collector cars in the garage. They wore the old man's tweedy hunting clothes, tight on Ray. With his double-bill hunting hat cocked to the side, José was Sherlock Homeboy.

"Takin the car is too much, I think," Ray said.

"Ray, let me explain somepin to you. We're criminals by need, not choice, see? I didn't make the world, son. I'm just makin it better, evenin it out, spread—"

"Spreadin the wealth, I know, I know. Then if you're keepin the car, I'm takin the dog."

José smacked the car roof. "You're *not* takin the dog. By the smell of tomorrow's breakfast, we got twenty whore dogs gonna show up from the Ten Mile woods, goddam hairy midgets. I'm not havin that nasty-lookin bastard in my house. Wolf. Look at 'im. He'll need to eat a cow every day to stay alive. Git out." José yanked the dog out of the backseat.

The dog ran around the car, hopped back in from the other side, tail stump a-wag.

"He's not comin, Ray."

"*C'mawn*. Look at his nails, man!"

"What about 'em?"

"They're crazy long, means he never gets walked or exercised. All that eye gunk, dry coat, never gets brushed. They dump cheap food in his bowl, that's all they do for him, he lets himself out the doggy door, starved for attention. Kinda life is that?"

"I ain't listenin." José stuck his fingers in his ears.

"Leavin him and that other one alone all weekend."

"Lalalalalalalaaaa."

"No dog sitter, not enough food or water, locked in the damn greenhouse, shit and piss all over the floor. These people are the devil's hands."

"They're smart. If they left 'em in the house there'd be shit and piss on the rugs. They're *dogs,* man. They did fine out there."

"Until you killed one. Murderer."

"The dog was attackin me, man! Why you gotta sweat me so, son? First it's gettin me out on the goddam river—"

"*Nin*ja Man!"

"*Squir*rel Boy!"

Ray petted the dog. "J? Go to hell."

"I'm plannin on it, the fun part, where they keep the whores, booze and pizza."

"I'm still takin this dog with us. Don't even try to stop me. After what you done to the first pup, you owe me."

"If I owe anybody it's the dead dog."

"I'm not leavin this other dog here behind on his lonesome."

José threw up his hands. "Hell with it. So take 'im. I don't know who's uglier, you or him."

Ray kissed the dog, let the dog lick his lips.

"That is true blue foul." José pissed into a garbage can. "Know where his mouth's been, prob'ly?"

"Lappin clean white snow."

"You keep tellin yourself that. Wind up with green mushrooms growin off your lips tomorrow." José plunked onto the tailgate to change out of the old man's slippers into the old man's tennis shoes. The toes of his left foot were black and gray.

"Damn, J-man. You're frostbit."

"Yeah, but it's gettin better. It don't even hardly hurt no more."

"J, listen. I think we might oughta go see Doc."

José squinted at his toes. "You're tellin me they ain't comin back then?"

"Let's let Doc have a look-see is all I'm sayin. Damn, man. J, I'm, like, I'm sorry, man."

"Say sorry again and I'll kill you."

"Can't say sorry, can't say thank you, anything I can say?"

"That you'll leave that goddam dog here."

"No."

José nodded. "To Doc's, then." He went to the driver-side door.

"Your foot, man. I can drive."

"It's my left foot's hurt. Right's fine. Think I'm gonna let you drive? You'll drive us off a cliff to avoid hittin a snow-flake. Git in."

Ray slumped into the backseat to be with the dog.

"Where to, Miss Daisy?" José said. "Look at 'im poutin. The hell's wrong now?"

"Serious? You wanna know?"

"Am I gonna be sorry I asked? I am, I can tell. Here it comes. Shit."

"Right about now I'm wonderin if there's anybody up there that cares a whit about us."

"You have got to be shittin me. What, like, is there a God who got your back, you're sweatin?"

"Damn straight."

"*I* got your back. Idiot. What else you need?" José fired up the engine. "Squirrels beware."

15

HOSPITALS ASKED TOO many questions. Doc worked on the down low.

He lived out back of a liquor store, lost his license for doing surgery drunk. Rumor was he amputated the wrong leg of some guy with bone cancer. José sat on his good foot as Doc gave him Valium and vodka, shot his bad foot with Novocain. He almost didn't feel Doc cutting away his toes.

"In a month you'll be running," Doc said. "You may have a pimp limp."

"I pimp limp any damn way, Doc." José tried not to grimace.

Doc sipped vodka between cuttings, nodded to Ray. "Squeeze your friend's hand to steal the pain off his foot. Squeeze his fingers hard."

Ray did.

"Damn, son, leggo my paw," José said. "Never mind m' toes, you're crushin m' fingers. Vise grip he's got there, Doc."

"I'm strong as hell sometimes," Ray said.

"I guess you are sometimes, then," José said.

"I'm guessing by the sound of those coughs," Doc said, "you both have something horrible in your lungs. On that shelf over there is a box full of antibiotics. Grab yourselves a fistful each."

Ray poked through a dusty box. "All I see is rotgut brandy."

"In the box next to the brandy, but take a bottle of that too."

Ray found packets labeled BAYTRIL—CANINE. "Says here this is for dogs, Doc."

"It's all the same stuff."

"Says here it's expired."

"It should still work." Doc stitched José's foot.

They paid Doc with diamond earrings stolen from the mansion. José limped because he was getting used to his new balance. Ray limped because he felt bad he could walk when José couldn't.

They went straight from Doc's to Frankie the Fence's, unloaded the Mercedes and the rest of their booty. While José negotiated prices with Frankie, Ray read to the Dobie from a book he swiped from the Jersey mansion. This dude Siddhartha said life is suffering. The news got worse: You never escaped it, even when you died. You came back in another body to a more rotten situation or, rarely, a slightly cooler one based upon your previous actions. This was karma. Basically, you got back what you gave, good and bad. Being a thief was crappy karma, the book said.

"Let's go, Ray-Ray." José fanned himself with six thousand dollars, let Ray roll him out of Frankie's shop in the secondhand wheelchair Frankie threw into the deal. "Six grand and a don't-rate wheelchair for a Mercedes and all that bling," José said.

"Frankie got to eat too, poor bastard, one leg four inches shorter than the other."

"Yo?" José said.

"Yeah?"

"We got six grand!"

"I know!"

Out on the sidewalk the boys hugged and howled in the dawn light until scavenger Richie darted out of the alley behind the methadone clinic next door, gun drawn.

"Guess you're not here to give us the other three bucks you owe us," José said.

Richie grabbed the boys' roll, ran.

"Why the city got to put a methadone clinic next to a pawn shop?" José said. "That is just ass-out bad urban planning."

Ray took stock: a lame old Doberman and two kids with pneumonia, one with half a foot gone, huddling to fight off the twelve-degree wind gutting the street, two hundred eighty bucks to their names. Ray nodded. "That right there was karma."

"No, that right there was my Ninja," José said. "Thank God I'm still chill on Valium, or I'd be bawlin right now." He was bawling.

The new dog fit right in with the Ten Mile pack.

"Quit that racket, dag dogs!" José had gritted out a month of bed rest by way of brandy, soup, and mutt medicine, but he was sick of being in bed smothered by the dogs who had come back at the smell of the first soup and who had nothing better to do all day than bug him.

Ray was working for a furniture mover, six bucks an hour but cash, no questions. The boss worked him like a freebie mule. His back and knees ached. Maybe he caused José to lose his toes. Maybe the junkies never would have picked the empty Ten Mile basement as their leaving Earth spot if the boys had been here to defend the house instead of in jail. Either way, watching the J-man loaf in front of the TV after a long day of humping couches up five flights of stairs was getting a little harder each night. Most annoying, the J-man gave running commentary on everything that flashed the TV. "Ever notice how commercials for feminal products got a light trombone soundtrack? I got a sneakin suspicion the news might be real sometimes. If cartoons of human people got four fingers, shouldn't cartoons of dog people got three?"

The Fatty dog settled in front of the TV, looked at José from the sides of its eyes.

"Move, dog!"

The new Dobie came and sat with Fatty, yawned. "Dog gumbo," José said. "Just you watch. I get back on my feet, there's gonna be some changes around here. You too."

"Hell'd I do but be your step-'n'-fetch every minute the last month?"

"Sick of your mopin around. Look at you, you girl. Your hair all long and kinked like a cavewoman. Go on and get yourself a haircut."

The boys eyed each other.

For a second Ray dared to dream that Yolie would rehire him, until he remembered he had just up and disappeared on her, no letter from jail to let her know he wouldn't be back. He didn't dare dream what Trini thought of him.

The teakettle whistled, Ray dumped hot water into a soup cup, served José.

"You really wanna help me, Ray-Ray, you'll put this fat dope dog out the house. Them sideways looks." José shivered. "He'll make a nice roast when we run outta money. Git him outta my *Tee*Vee line." José threw a pair of balled socks at the dog. The socks bounced off the dog's head. The dog didn't move. José threw a blanket over the dog, put his feet up on Fatty. "Good footstool at least. Bring me a beer, son, and let's see what's on the cartoon channel."

"You're milkin this foot thing pretty good."

"It *hurts,* man."

"Wonder how them blue folks are makin out about now."

"Ray? Please. For like half a hour, stop thinkin so much. You think you could do that for fifty minutes? Your mind is a mystery of frights to me."

"Think they're still stuck together?"

"Son, leave them poor blue folks be and toss me the goddam TV clicker."

A week later José was at his crossword book, the kind for second graders. He figured if he was going to become a first-rate criminal, he at least would have to know how to forge bank checks. He licked his pencil. "Yo son, the word *scream*? Where's the *3* go?"

"What?"

"The letter *3*. After the *k,* right?"

And this guy wants me to go off on my own? No way. We're friends to the ends, dying together at good old Ten Mile River. "Sure, put the *3* after the *k*."

"Took you long enough."

Ray checked the Helps in the local Spanish paper for shady moving companies, saw none. The guy he had been working for skipped town with his last week's pay. Ray shook the money can, nickels and pennies, no paper. "My dogs are two days from starvation."

"Time to start stealin," José said.

"You got one foot."

José stood, limped around. "I am one out-of-shape thief."

"This is endless," Ray said.

"What is?"

"Nothin to look forward to."

"Fix for that one? Stop lookin forward. Mopey-ass woman. Are you cryin?"

"I got allergies, okay? Shut up."

"Allergies. Sure. A'right, Ray, look, no need to panic, Papi got this all figured out. Till I'm able to run, we're gonna shape up with the Mexicans up on 179th there, by the bridge."

"The day workers lookin for pickup gigs? That's hard work."

"For hard men." José pounded his chest, coughed, winked.

At sunrise they waited on the corner of 179th and Saint Nick with some fifty illegals, mostly Mexican. No one talked. A Russian in a flatbed pickup with DRAGO DEMOLITION hand painted on the side pulled up to the corner and yelled in bad Spanish he was paying three bucks an hour for hump work.

The Mexicans nodded. They didn't look happy or sad.

Ray and José were the tallest and youngest of the men, and the Russian picked them first. A friendly-looking white dude reached down from the back of the truck, gave Ray and José a hand and swung them up into the flatbed. "Breon," he said with a wink.

"'Ey," the boys said.

"Welcome." The Breon cat clapped their backs, nodded that they should sit on a blanketed bench in the front of the pickup bed, reached down to help the others into the truck.

The Drago punk poked his finger at one last man, shoved back the others. "No máz. I am need only seven. No máz!"

One of the left-back men, an old-timer, pulled a sandwich from his coat, gave it to a younger man in the truck, kissed the man's cheek. Ray watched those left behind get smaller as the truck roared away west onto the George Washington Bridge. The truck banged over a pothole, threw everybody around the truck bed.

Breon nudged Ray. "Tay?"

"Huh?"

Breon unscrewed a thermos, poured tea into tiny paper cups for Ray, José and the other men, sucked in a draft of the cold wind blasting the bridge. "Gargeous marnin, ay fellers?" Breon was thirty or so with a killer smile. "Crisp."

Ray found himself smiling, looked at José, also smiling. Ray shrugged.

◆

"What you thinkin?"

"I'm thinkin how you gonna lug junk all day on half a foot."

"Ray, don't worry so much, a'right? Relax?"

The Drago cat pointed to a pile of rubble in the back of the condo site, pointed to a Dumpster. "You put *that* in *there*. *Ponga eso allí.* You gan understand me? *Comprende?*"

The boys nodded.

By lunch José was friends with everyone on the job. Drago chucked the men bananas—lunch—talked with the construction foreman, who said, "You wanna do this here?"

"Except for Irish over there, they don't speak English. Irish is alright."

"What do I owe you?" the foreman said.

Drago said, "Seven man times eleven hour at fifteen a head and then me at twenty-five an hour."

"So what is that?" the foreman said, reaching into his pocket for cash.

"Sixteen seventy-five," Drago said.

"Fourteen thirty," Ray said, his mouth full of banana.

The construction foreman took out his phone, worked it up on the calculator. "Fourteen thirty." He eyed Drago.

Drago eyed Ray.

Breon nudged Ray, nodded, smiled. "That's a good lad."

◆

After lunch Drago picked José for light duty, pulling nails from two-by-fours. Ray humped junk to dusk. José waved to Ray. Ray flipped off José.

The truck dumped them at 179th with thirty-three bucks each, Drago keeping the rest. Breon said, "I give yas a lift home?"

"We're a'right," José said.

"You've been limping all day, friend José. C'mon, little brother."

They walked to a parking garage, picked up Breon's car, a black Lexus convertible, the kind you can't drive when you're making three dollars an hour. The boys stared at Breon.

"I'm a saver." Breon winked. "Hop in." He showed them all the bells and whistles on the ride south, stereo booming rap, heated seats; demonstrated the souped-up engine with pedal-to-the-metal acceleration down Riverside. Ray smiled, looked at José. José winked at Ray. The boys clutched their stomachs, screamed laughter.

Ray threw his head back. Dizzied by the blue sky, clean wind in his hair, he thought he was as happy as he'd ever been, for a few seconds.

"Like bein roller-coaster drunk," José yelled over the wind. "We're over here." He pointed to a city housing building off Riverside.

Breon skidded in front of the tenement. "Nice workin with yas. Here." He gave them a box of cookies.

"Nah, that's a'right," José said.

"Take 'em, please. And take my number." He handed them a card, winked, drove off. His card had a number, no name, no address.

"We live here now, huh?" Ray said.

"I don't want him knowin about Ten Mile."

"He's real nice. I like him a ton."

"Me too," José said. "But drivin that ride, he's one to watch out for." He waved to Breon, rounding the corner. "*Damn,* that is one hot car."

"Hot-lookin or—"

"Both."

16

SUNDAY MORNING CAME a perfect day, spring's messenger. They hung at the bridge but no one came by looking for day workers. On the walk home the air was sweet with tree bud, melting snow, cheap perfume rising off the necks of girls not wearing jackets to show off their spring clothes. José wasn't wearing a jacket either. He took off his shirt.

"Jesus," Ray said.

Back at the stationhouse José got the TV going, Ray cleaned. "You can't help me clean for half an hour?"

"I don't mind the mess."

"*I* do."

"Then *you* clean it."

Ray chucked his dish towel. "I'm bored. You bored?"

José was lost in his Grand Theft game. "Huh?"

"Too nice a day for a man to stay inside the house. Let's do somepin."

"Nailed him! Damn, son, you see that head shot! I am gettin so good at this level, I'm gonna be in level nine by nightfall! Hooooooo! I can't believe it! I can't *believe* it! My talent frightens me sometimes."

Ray grabbed his board, headed out.

"Where you goin?" José said.

Ray eyed José. "Haircut."

José sighed, nodded. "Had to happen sometime."

"You comin?"

"Not unless you got a extra bulletproof vest."

Ray kicked his board down the street, the melting ice running rivers to the gutters, wiped out face to pavement in front of Yolanda's Braid Palace. Covered in slush he slumped into the shop like a man marching himself to the electric chair. From the look of the line of punks in there, forget about the braids, the business was haircuts for horn-dogs now.

Yolie saw Ray in the doorway, his do-rag lost in the fall from his skateboard, his long red hair standing off his head like match flame in a windstorm. She dropped her shears, put her hands to her mouth. She was shaking. "Amor. *Qué pasó?* Oh mi amor. What happened to you?"

Ray nodded. "Missis Yolie."

Yolie shook her head. She turned to the chairs doubled

up with horny teenagers, clapped her hands for them to git. "Vayan," she said. Even when she was upset, her voice was soft. "Everybody out. Yolie closing early today."

"That ain't fair," and "This is *bull*shit," and "C'*mawn*, man," came back at her.

She shooed them out the door. They filed out, giving Ray kill you eyes. A defiant pipsqueak in a booster seat hung back in the barber chair.

Yolie glared at him, crossed her arms, tapped her foot.

The scrawny kid squeaked to Yolie's tetas, "I ain't hardly just sat down."

"Easy, Junior." Yolie took the kid's chin in her hand and raised it and the little squeaker's eyes away from her breasts. "Tomorrow, you first on line." Yolie spun the barber chair and helped the pipsqueak down from it. The kid backed out of the shop, tripped backward up the steps. Ray chuckled. He remembered what it was like being a goddam kid.

Yolie flipped the sign to CLOSED, locked the door, glared at Ray, tapped her foot.

"Sorry," Ray said.

"Why?"

"Like, because I feel bad—"

"Why did you *disappear*? There's only one reason gonna get you out of this one."

"It's that," Ray said.

"You couldn't call me, amor? You couldn't let me know?

Amor, amor, amor, I don't know what to do with you."

Ray gulped. "How's the Enrique franchise doin, ma'am?"

"I sold it to a muñeca in Brooklyn. Sure, now you're disappointed." She rattled off in furious Spanish at him for a minute, wore herself out, pulled him into a hug, stroked his hair. "Leave it long, amor. We braid it and bead it."

"Nah, it's gonna get hot, ma'am. Spring comes, a man needs short hair."

"Amor, amor. Ay. Where you living now?"

"We're fine, ma'am."

"So the José is still alive too, eh?" She combed back Ray's hair with her fingers. "I think you got taller. Your eyes too, something new there."

"Don't cry, ma'am."

Yolie hurried away to the stairs. "Trini, what you doing up there, amor?"

"Homework," Trini yelled down.

"Your friend is here."

"My friend?"

"Su ángel. Ha vuelto."

"Who, you mean—ohmygod." The ceiling shook with the sound of running feet. "José?"

"No," Yolie said. "The other one."

"Raymond," Ray whispered. He saw Trini's feet at the top of the stairs.

"Tell him to go away," Trini said.

"Amor, come down here," Yolie said.

"I got *home*work, Tía. I don't have *time* to waste on—"

Yolie smacked the railing. *"Trini, ven aquí ahorita."*

Yolie went upstairs to let them work it out on their own.

The warm air rolled through the shop window, but Trini still wore her winter sweater. Her hands were cold as she forced Ray's head forward and drove the buzzer over his scalp. "I would've visited, you know."

"The visiting room, it ain't like the movies. It's sadder and louder."

"I know sad and loud."

"Not like this."

Trini pulled Ray's head back and cranked the buzzer. "Not even a letter."

"I know. That was bad."

"Bad? I'm liable to dig the brains out of your head with this here clipper. How many weeks I'm going down to the godforsaken shack there, peeking in the windows for y'all, joint is empty, the dogs gone. Thought y'all died or something, ran away. I didn't know what to think. I'm like, why'd they ditch me? What've I done? What, I stink or something?"

"You stink beautiful, like coconut bubble gum plus salt."

"Shut up. Tt, see what you made me do?" Trini put a tissue to Ray's scalp where she'd scraped it. "I smell like *salt*?"

"Salt's my favorite smell."

"Salt doesn't smell."

"How's your cousin?"

"I hate you."

"We figured we only knew you for a month—"

"Five weeks. A lot can happen in five weeks. A lot did happen. I'm not just talking about your bato friend there, the dawg, I'm talking you and me. We could talk, you know? Or maybe that was just me. Maybe I thought we were friends. Maybe I'm stupid."

"Trini, yo, sorry. For real. I didn't know you, you know, felt like that."

"Y'all were just messin with me, I guess. Y'all boys, I'll never understand a one of you. I should go nun myself right now and get it over with. Hold still."

"Sure, just maybe could you go a little easier with that clipper there? No? Okay, I don't mind. I'll bleed to death for the cause—whoa. I gotta be hemorrhaging after that one."

"I wish we never met."

Ray watched Trini in the mirror. She was a full woman. She had a perfect butt. "You think your aunt would go out with me?"

Trini spun the chair to face Ray. "Raymond, are you okay?"

"Me? Like, whaddaya mean?"

"I mean, like, after jail and all. I don't like to think about it. What they do to you in there."

"Nah, nah, hell, it was nothin. It's not as bad as the movies."

"You just said it was worse." She took off her sweater.

Ray saw her underwear just above her jeans when her shirt came up with the sweater. He forced his eyes away, couldn't help himself, peeked again, but by now Trini had pulled down her shirt.

"We still friends?" he said.

"No, and you turn your head again while I'm clippin and I'll make you van Gogh."

"How was I supposed to write you to tell you I got pinched for car theft after I just promised you, like, I wasn't thieving anymore? I was embarrassed."

"Being embarrassed is better than being thoughtless."

"Well, even if you ain't friends with me anymore, I'm still friends with you."

"You can't do that. You can't be friends with somebody if they don't wanna be friends back."

"Oh, don't worry. I won't bother you. You won't even notice me. I'll just be friends with you in my heart is all."

Trini stopped shaving his head. "What?"

"Nothin. I'm fifteen now."

"So?" She started buzzing his scalp again.

"Y'all probly turned seventeen, huh?"

"Still sixteen."

"Cool. I'm catchin up."

"You make me so mad."

"Ouch. José misses you."

"Ha."

"He wants to come uphill and drop a hi on you."

"That dawg can stay where he is, I'm just fine, thank you, got me a nice man now at school."

"The hell you do."

"The hell I *do*." She snapped her fingers Miss Thing style.

Ray scrunched his lips and eyes. "He older than you?"

"Who, him? Yeah, he is." Trini lifted her chin high. "He's eighteen."

Ray sat up. Dag. Prob'ly shaves like at least twice a week. "He's gonna start losin his hair, you gonna have a bald-head man. That's when it starts, the baldness, eighteen. You get a look at the top of his head?"

She didn't say anything.

"Yup."

"Ttt." She was about to slap the top of his head, stopped, rested her hand on his scalp as if palming a basketball, stole his breath. She rested her hand on his shoulder. "Raymond, what are you doing?" she said to his reflection.

"Me? What I did? I ain't doin nothin."

"Why'd you come back here?"

Ray stared at her, looked away. "I missed everybody is all, like."

"Raymond?"

"Yeah?"

"Ray?"

Not Raymond but *Ray.* What did that mean? "Still here."

"You know the day's coming, right? At some point, you gotta move on, you know? Look at me. A special school. We'll find one for you. Filled with kids like you. Special kids."

"Freaks, you mean."

"Special *folks* who'll help you find what you love."

I know what I love, he almost said.

"Raymond, he wants you to go too. He told me one time. He said, 'I'm gonna get rich and send Ray to an Ivy Leaf college.'"

"Ivy Leaf. José kills me."

"Yeah." Trini caught herself wearing a dreamy smile, killed it, slapped the top of Ray's head.

"Forgot you was mad at me, huh?" Ray said. "Yo, woman, we still friends or what?"

"I gotta think about it."

"Take your time, you done thinkin about it yet?"

She squinted at him by way of the wall mirror. She pecked the top of his shaved head. "Okay, but no José. Not yet."

Her kiss electrocuted him. From beyond the grave he said, "Okay, you let me know when you're ready, then. About José, I mean."

"Promise me you'll never steal again."

He turned around in the chair to face her. "Trini, I swear to God. Even though I'm not sure I believe in God anymore. Tell you what, I swear to you."

"Please don't break my heart."

17

"SHE'S OUTTA HER mind," José said. "Stop stealin? How's a man opposed to eat?"

"We're workin pickups, man. We be a'right."

"That's short-term, partner. Think Scarface is gonna hump junk the rest of his life? Soon's my foot's better, I'm back in action. How'd she look, though?"

Like I'd trade death for a kiss. "She looked a'right. You know, same."

"Thinks I'm gonna quit thievin for her? That's more than a lifestyle change. That's swappin out bones. *Hell* with 'er."

"I'm likin the idea that Yolie said she'd train us to cut heads. Earn while we learn style. Hell's wrong with that?"

"I ain't workin in no *braid* shop, son."

"I think I'd like it."

"Then you go do it. Me, I'm a man. I need a man's work. Dag, hair cuttin? That's girls' truck, son."

"You never seen a barber?"

"Barberin is old men's work. Plus I ain't goin near Yolie's shop, work or not. Trini's liable a grab a shears and stab me on sight."

"She'll yell at y'all for an hour and then you'll be back in there. You gotta get up there quick, drop a hi on her. Look, I ain't know how to say this."

"Say it."

"She got a new man. He's eighteen."

José's eyes went wide. He recovered. "Psh, good for her. Psh. Like I care. Psh."

"J, she still likes you. I can tell. It's not too late."

"Nah. I'm over her, man." José chewed a cornrow tail, spit it out. "Eighteen. Psh. Loser be goin bald soon."

"I told her."

They shaped up with a bunch of pickup outfits through April until big brother Breon hooked them up with a Senegalese who took a liking to them and offered them steady work with his landscaping company, six bucks an hour to pull dandelions out of rich folks' New Jersey lawns. Sundays off, Ray hung out with Trini. One weekend they went to the zoo.

"Y'all ready to come on down Ten Mile way, drop a hi on my boy?" Ray said.

"He wanna see me so bad, he can come uphill to me, I don't care one way or another if he does or not." Trini reached into the paper bag of feed she'd bought for the petting zoo animals, brought some cracked corn to her lips.

Ray stopped her, gave her his bag of peanuts. "You were wantin these, no?"

Trini pouted, stomped ahead, came back, grabbed Ray's arm, huffed, "Let's go, Mr. Slow."

And then Ray went home and said, "Go see her, man."

"Ray, shut up about her, will ya? I don't even think about her no more. Here's a idea for ya. *You* take her."

"Psh, like I would." If only I could.

One day their boss Mr. Okolo sent them to meet up with Breon at a penthouse terrace on the Upper West Side.

On their way down Central Park West they passed a fancy school, JENNINGS PREPARATORY said the cut marble over the entrance. Ray pretended to be surprised. "Yo, that's Trini's school."

"Who, Trini's? Serious? Dag. C'mon, we're gonna be late for work."

"Maybe we'll come this way on the way back," Ray said.

"Nah. Maybe. Nah."

"Maybe."

"Nah."

◆

The miniature poodle ran out onto the penthouse terrace to interrupt the boys' lunch break, pulled on José's cuff to show the J-man how it liked to lick its butt.

"I dunno how they can like to lick their butts so much," José said.

"They dunno how you can't," Breon said with a wink between Marlboro puffs.

Ray nodded. That kind of funny thrilled Ray. Not hee-haw humor but quiet, smart funny.

Breon was smart all right, treating the boys to thick steak sandwiches, gourmet potato chips and fancy soda that must have cost him half his day's wages. Ray wondered what Breon wanted.

"Say, fellas," Breon said as he and the boys munched their sandwiches, "you've had a chance to get a look at the penthouse, have yas?"

José swallowed his sandwich. "Real nice place."

Ray sipped his soda. "Swank as hell."

"Sure. Yas see the kid's room there, off the back hall there, past the bath-a-room there?"

Ray shook his head, not to say no, but because he knew what was coming.

"That Macintosh laptop on the kid's desk there. It's a Macbook Pro, don't you know. All them peripherals. Three gigs of RAM, don't you know." Breon's three came out *tree*. Ray thought that was so cool. "A man could take down the world with that machine. Don't ya tink, José?"

José didn't know crap about computers. He bit into his sandwich, squinted. "So what are you sayin?"

"I'm saying I get a magazine that tells me that machine retails for seven tousand dollars."

José looked at Ray. "So that's what he's sayin."

Ray liked Breon, but he didn't want to screw over Mr. Okolo. Just last week Mr. O had given the boys a stereo, his kid's throwaway to make room for a better one, but it was nice. "Breon—"

"I'm not saying anything anyway. Or maybe I'm saying this: I work for a couple of fancy landscaping companies that get me into these palaces here. I'm saying I can get you boys in with me, into these companies. Into these palaces. I'm saying we're brothers."

"Sure, with that pink skin you wear there, we're brothers," José said.

"Brother," Breon said, lighting José a fresh Marlboro, "don't you know the Mickies are the slaves of Europe? Like it or not, we're brothers thick. See now, I always wanted kid brothers."

And they had always wanted an older brother, one with a cool accent and a killer smile that made you forget what you wanted to say. Who was *so* cool he could make you almost want to steal a laptop with him, even when you had sworn to the love of your life you were doing your damnedest to stay clean. Breon would be a millionaire with a swank joint in Bermuda before he was thirty-five, and the boys knew it. Maybe he'll take us with him, Ray thought, then hated himself for thinking it.

"Look, yas don't trust me yet. That's fine too. Nobody with half a head trusts anybody anyway." Breon fed the boys fresh boxes of Marlboro 100s. "All I'm saying is, I'm tinkin that Mac there on the kid's desk is a cool computer." Cool came out *coal*.

Yeah, Ray thought, Breon is coal.

18

"THINK HE TOOK it?" Ray said.

The boys walked up Central Park West after work. Mr. O gave them the afternoon off to enjoy the weather.

"He'll give the doorman a grand to take it while the rich folks is on vacation. That's what I'd do anyhow." José tapped his head. "I can't help it, my criminal mind. It just keeps feedin me the ideas. Natural born thief, son. Ah well, we all got our gifts."

"We best keep to our plant waterin."

"For the time bein." José smacked Ray's dome. "I tell you, I like Breon's style. Quiet. Don't trust him farther than I can piss, but I like him fine. I'm-a partner up with him soon's my foot's a hundrit percent." He smacked Ray's head again.

"Will you quit hittin me?"

"It's fun."

"*Knew* you was gonna get in on it with Breon. You're on your own."

"I ain't tryin a make you come with me, Ray. I'm happier you don't."

Ray stopped José. "I'm not lettin you do it."

"Oh really? Who the fuck are you? Mind your truck, I mind mine."

"You can't do that to Mr. O. You steal from someplace Mr. O sent you—"

"I ain't gonna do it to Mr. O, Ray. I'm not a asshole. Only guys like Drago. Think I'd do that to Mr. O?" José gave Ray mean eyes, walked ahead.

"Then what about you? Gettin pinched?"

"I won't."

"Hey, J, you're an idiot, man."

José spun back, grabbed Ray's shirt. "Grow up, son. Get gone. Serious. Sick a hangin around wif you. Goddam *kid*. Get lost."

"The hell *you* doin here?" someone yelled from across the street.

The boys spun, saw Trini march down the Jennings School steps, through the crowd of kids dressed in their plaid skirts and blazers, bopping their heads to iPods, spinning BlackBerry wheels.

At the sight of her José dropped his filthy knapsack, pimp limped across the street, met her on the sidewalk, arms wide, hands dirty from planting flowers, reaching out to her. "Yo, baby."

Trini reared back and slapped José with a right hook that made his head wobble.

The rich kids said *Dag* and *Snap* and *Du-hude, that was a shot*.

Some movie star–looking cat with sideburns, a wispy goatee and fake messy hair came down the stairs on a run, jerked Trini's arm. "Who's he?"

"Back off, Richard," Trini said. "This doesn't concern you."

The Richard cat shoved José. "Fuck is your problem, homeboy?"

"Stop, Richard!" Trini said.

Ray gunned it across the street, got in Richard's face. "You step to my boy, you step to me."

"I got it, Ray," José said.

"Who's this Lurch now? Another one of your uptown peoples, Trin?"

"Raymond, don't," Trini said.

Trini's man spun back to José. "Who are you to be all up on my girl, man?"

Trini pushed her man off. "Back up, Richard. He's—"

"I'm not talking to you," Richard said to Trini. "I'm talking to him." He turned to José. "Yo, you deaf, homeboy? I said, what's up with you getting all in my girl's business and shit?"

Trini finger-popped in front of Richard's face. "Hel*lo*! He's just a friend." She snap-turned to José. "Hell am I saying? You're no friend."

"Yeah, huh?" Richard said. "Then what exactly is he?"

José laughed. "Chill, man. C'mon now. We're men here. Let's talk this out, bro."

"Talk what out?" Trini said.

"'Bro,' you're calling me? You're not my *bro,* bro." The loser tugged on his goatee, flicked his cigarette at José.

Richard's boys circled José and Ray. A crowd gathered to watch the coming brawl.

"Dude, why don't you just head on back uptown or wherever your slick ass comes from and leave my girl be?"

"Your *girl*?" Trini said. "Your *girl*?"

"I'd call you a slut, except you're a prude," Richard said.

Ray blew back Richard with a stiff arm. He knocked down two of Richard's posse with shoves. The rest of the kids set upon Ray and José.

Ray heard his name, an anguished cry. "Raymond, please! Ray, stop!"

He stopped, looked around, Richard's posse on their backs, Ray and José standing. Stunned, José stared at Ray.

"Stop!" Trini said. "Just everybody stop. Please." She turned to José. "I'm sorry. I'm sorry I hit you." She reached out to touch his face, but when he reached out to her, she pulled back. Sobbing, she hurried to the subway.

The Richard cat dusted himself off, made his way down the steps to the curb and a waiting limo. "Take her, Paco. She's all hand, no suck."

Ray eyed the remaining kids. *"Git,"* he said.

The kids scattered.

On the subway home José said, "Somethin happened to you in that juvie run."

Ray had been sucked into a book called *A Brief History of Time*. It said the universe started out smaller than an atom. By the time it finished expanding, one atom would be bigger than the present-day universe. "I grew."

"I don't think so," José said. "But you *look* like you grew." José winked, chicked his cheek, Breon Junior. "You beat up half the high school there, Ray. You might just be a badass."

"I wanna be a goodass."

"Ass ass."

"Tryin a read, man. Hush." Ray flipped the page.

"Tellin me to hush. Yo? Fine, be that way, geek." José sighed, took out his motorcycle magazine, all pictures, bit off from the bar of chewing tobacco Breon had given him. "I'd cut both my arms off to hold Trini's hand again."

The book said time travel was real. You could travel to the future but not to the past. Too bad. Ray wanted to go back to the day he introduced Trini to José, redo it. Undo it.

◆

That night came a knock on the stationhouse door. All hell broke loose with the dogs. The boys grabbed their baseball bats. "We're armed," José yelled.

The door opened, Trini came in. The dogs remembered her. She hugged and settled the pack, put a strand of hair into her mouth, chewed it as she looked at José. She went to him, buried her head in his neck, hid there. He put his arms around her.

Ray left, wondering how many minutes would pass before they would realize he'd gone.

19

BREON TOOK THEM to a crowded Starbucks after end-of-shift, bought the boys more than they could eat, told them to save a seat for him at the window, he had to hit the "canny."

Ray had begun wearing a spoon on a chain around his neck. He balanced the spoon crossways on his finger and stared at it.

"Damn spoon bendin," José said.

"I'm *so* close to bendin it."

"Ray, I'll be a respectable citizen before you bend any dag spoon." José grabbed the spoon, stuffed it into the trash. "Freak. Now where's my boy Breon at? I don't want to be here, rich losers swillin fancy drinks they can't pronounce, small coffee runs on the tag *tall* in this joint, psh. What's wrong wif Micky D's?"

Ray pulled his spoon from the trash.

"The dollar menu? Show me better value than the dollar menu, try to. Five bucks a damn cup a joe. That's like four chicken chimichangas and a fry."

"But Starbucks got good cookies."

José sighed. "They do, though. Their cookies are fierce. Here he is."

Breon came out of the bathroom. On his way to the window counter he grabbed a souped-up laptop from a table where some guy was way into a conversation on his mobile, his head turned to stare at the butt of the chick who had come out from behind the counter to sweep dust into her dustpan. Breon folded the laptop, tucked it under his arm, casually walked across Starbucks, slipped the laptop into Ray's knapsack. He even sat down and sipped his coffee.

"Hell'd you just do there, Breon?" Ray said.

"I think yous know what I just did. Right there in my little brother Ray's bag is a five-day trip to Disney World." Breon winked. "We've got ourselves about thirty seconds before pretty boy there figures out his laptop is gone. I'm tinkin we should probably leave. I'll go out the side door, yous go out the front. Nice and easy now, loved ones. Meet yas at the car."

"Breon, take that damn laptop out of my bag and give it back to . . ."

Breon was already on his way out.

"Dag," Ray said. "Should I give it back?"

"Too late for that. The mark's lookin all around now."

"He's panicked, J-man. Look at him."

"Don't look at him," José said. "Let's go. Yawn and walk real slow and scratch your head with one hand and your butt with the other, like you got nowheres to rush to. Make like me."

Outside they started over to Breon's car, stopped when they saw a cop talking to Breon, pointing to Breon's registration sticker. "Expired," the cop said.

Breon shook his head, grinned. "Bless me for a dullard, I forgot." He eyed the cop's cruiser. "Say, you're in the Two Four, are ya? Do you know Eamon Lafferty?"

"Not well enough for you to talk your way out of a two-hundred-dollar ticket. See some ID?"

"Positively, Officer." Breon pretended he didn't know the boys as they walked past the car to the uptown subway entrance.

José whispered, "Bet he talks himself out of the fine."

"My goddam knees are shakin. Gotta get this laptop out of my knapsack."

In the safety of the stationhouse the boys stared at the stolen computer. José rubbed his nose. "I don't see why folks spend six grand on a piece of plastic. Anyway, praise Jesus they do." José grabbed the laptop, headed for the door.

"Hell you doin?" Ray grabbed the laptop.

"Hell *you* doin? Gimme that thing. Frankie the Fence gonna open his night hours in twenty minutes, I wanna be first at the window, save me from hangin in line with all them jonesin crackheads. Ray, you're not seriously thinkin what I think you're thinkin?"

"Yup."

"You're not givin it back."

"Yup. Gonna mail it."

"Kid, a man's gotta eat."

"The guy's life is on here. His social, address, letters to his gal, his *ideas*."

"Ray-Ray, I'm your bud. It's my goddam duty to tell ya you're bein a asshole. Now, here's what's gonna happen. I'm gonna swing that thing, we're gonna split the bread with Breon."

"No you're not. I promised Trini."

"That's your problem. I didn't promise her nothin. Woman loves me as I am."

"You know she wants you to go clean, though. You *know* she does."

"Ray, you see my face, right?"

"Yup."

"You see I'm gettin serious mad, right?"

"Yup."

"Can you say any goddam thing but yup?"

"Nope."

"Ray, we can fence that thing for big money *because* the

guy's personal information is on it. Look, *I'm* gonna do it. Alone. Your word with Trini still be good, man. You didn't steal it. You don't gotta be involved."

"I'm involved."

"You're holdin my Ninja in your hand there. You're holdin two years' supply of dog food, how's that? Ray, gimme it!"

Ray jumped to the far side of the couch, José following, the boys circling.

"Look, man, I seen it on TV that *everybody*'s gonna get their ID swiped at some point," José said.

"Then let somebody else swipe it. We pitch that guy's life away on a stupid motorcycle and that's the beginnin of a forever badness. Leakin out that guy's soul to the world, man?"

"He's some rich-ass, Starbucks-swillin inheritor punk. He can afford it. He'll pay a lawyer to make things right. He'll prob'ly even figure out a way to *make* money off losin his ID. They all do, them rich folks. We're just evenin things out a little—"

"No we're not. Not today."

"Goddammit, Ray."

"I ain't puttin somethin that oily into motion, that guy's self gettin passed around and used in ten thousand online crimes. Only losers would do a forever lame thing. What you always told me? A good thief is hit and run, over and done."

"I did tell you that, I know. I like the way it rhymed good. Christ Jesus, where you goin with that thing now?"

"The river."

"You are not pitchin that machine into the mud-fucked Hudson. You are not. Hey!"

Ray ran out of the house, José after him, the dogs after José. At the riverside the dogs tripped Ray to play with him. He got up, coiled himself like a discus thrower, got the laptop off just as José tackled him . . .

Plunk.

"You fool! Man, Ray. Man!"

Huffing and puffing, the Fatty dog caught up with the pack, sat sideways next to José, looked at the J-man from the side of his eyes.

"You now." José looked out to where Ray had pitched the laptop. "This friendship is gettin costly."

They were drinking soup out of cans when the knock on the door came like a song, "Danny Boy."

"Uh-oh."

"Yup." José got the door. "You talked your way out of it, right?"

Breon showed José the ticket, no fine, just a warning. He gave José a six-pack of Bud. "Took me half an hour to cozy the cop, and then the traffic, New York, New York, it's a helluva town, sorry I took so long."

"Now how in hell did you figure where we live?" Ray said.

"All those times I drop yas off, yas never invite me up for a cup o' tay? Sure, I was a little hurt, a lot suspicious. Last time I dropped yas at the building there, I parked around the corner there, followed yas here. Is a man a man if he cares not where his brothers live?" Breon surveyed the rundown stationhouse from the door. He chuckled at the gigantic TV amidst the street-found furniture, smiled sadly as he took in the rest of the shabby house. "Ah, poor kids. Now I see why yas didn't want me to see where yas lived. Have you no parents?"

They shrugged. "Who needs 'em?" José said.

Right about now, we *need 'em,* Ray almost said.

"Boys, boys, brother Breon is gonna have you fellas out of here and livin the high life, don't you worry about it." Breon winked. "So, let's see our pretty little machine."

"Yeah, well, see, um, it's gone," José said. "Genius Ray here's gonna tell you all about it. Go 'head, genius Ray. All yours."

Breon scrunched his face, but he was still smiling, forever smiling. "What's this now?"

"C'mon in, Breon." José held the door wide for Breon.

Breon stepped over the threshold, grabbed himself a tallboy from the six he'd given José, cracked it, leaned back on the wall, cocked his head. "So?"

"I pitched it."

Breon laughed. He had a great laugh, loud, real, like José's. "No you didn't."

Ray pouted. "I had to."

"*Had* to? You *had* to pitch the machine I risked jail time for? That machine?"

The boys didn't say anything.

Breon plopped down onto the couch, folded his hands behind his head, propped his feet up on the Fatty dog. Fatty looked out the side of his eyes to see the thing that had put its feet on him.

"Please, man," Ray said. "Take your feet off the dog, man. He's old. He's half-blind, man. He gets nervous."

"I think you are scarin old Fatty a little there, Breon," José said. "I mean, I do it to the stupid summabitch all the time, but—"

"Ray," Breon said, "if you really did toss it, then I suppose you owe me a machine now. That one happened to run about six tousand dollars." He winked and *chick*-ed his cheek.

"Breon," José said. "Look, he's sorry."

"No I ain't," Ray said. "This ain't right."

"This is a serious matter, Ray. This is grave. See, here's the problem." Breon whipped out a butterfly knife and whittled the landscaping dirt out of his fingernails. "I kind of don't believe you're tat stupid to trow away a laptop. I tink you're holdin out on me, after all those lunches I bought you, the cigs—"

"You got us the lunch and cigs on your own," Ray said. His voice was louder than he expected.

"Easy, Ray," José said. "We're all pals here."

"We didn't ask for none of that stuff."

"But you took it, didn't you?" Breon sipped his beer.

"We didn't ask you to steal no laptop either."

"Ray, chill," José said.

Breon shifted his feet on Fatty's head. Fatty shivered under the weight of Breon's steel-plate combat boots.

"Get your goddam feet off my dog."

Breon's eyes flashed for a second, but his smile never left him. "That's some unfriendly talk there, Ray." He whittled away at his thumbnail and whistled. "Ray, be a good boy and get me the laptop. I'm countin to ten—"

"And I'm countin to five." Ray exploded, tears from nowhere. "Five, four—"

"One, two—"

"Three," both said.

"*Chill,* Ray," José said. "Yo, Breon. It's gone. For real. We trashed it."

"*We* now, is it?"

Fatty whimpered.

"Breon," Ray said. "You're *hurtin* him."

"We'll get you another laptop, B," José said. "Serious. We have it to you by tomorrow, word is bond. Me and my moron brother here. Lemme show you my Grand Theft skills, man. We play getaway partners, make Ray the cop, kick his ass."

"You're a cutie, José, but here's another lesson for ya: Ya can't charm a charmer. Get. Me. My. Laptop."

The Fatty dog yelped.

Ray pulled at Breon's leg.

Breon was up fast, the knife twinkling as it whirled in his hand. He whipped his arm so fast Ray didn't see the knife sweep his chest, but he felt it.

Ray looked down at his T-shirt, cut in the baggy part under the chest, at the ribs. He parted the rip. His skin was clean.

"Ray, I'm fond of ya. I am. But next time, I have to nick you, see? Get my computer, or I'll stab your dog, your José, and then you." He winked.

"Breon."

Breon and Ray turned to José.

José reached into the toaster oven, pulled out a gun. "Y'all best mosey now."

Breon shut one eye and squinted the other at the gun. "I bet it's a toy."

"Bet all you want." José cocked the trigger, winked.

Breon nodded, smiled as he headed for the door. "Fellas, enjoy the beer." He halted at the door. "And I really do hope you didn't kill that laptop. Not for me, but for you. There was money in that thing, boys. Real money that could have taken you places." He left, halted at José's voice.

"Just in case y'all think of dropping in on us again—"

"Like while yas are sleepin, for instance, my razor drawn? Yas can't stay awake forever."

José smiled. He nodded to Ray. "Let's us introduce Breon to our roommates."

Ray yelled out the open window, "Yo *dawgs*!"

Every last mangy, ragged pit bull ran uphill into the house, settled at Ray's feet, the giant Dobie between Ray's legs.

"Say hullo to our lil' friends," José said in his best Scarface voice.

Breon kept his cool, his eyes just a bit wider. He smiled, backed out of the house until he got far enough uphill, turned around and disappeared in the weed trees, his smile gone.

"You wet your pants a little, Ray."

Ray checked. José was right, a flower at the crotch. "Think he'll be back with his posse? You know them Irish."

José squinted. "I figure Breon for the loner type. He don't run with nobody. He's too cool to run with other folks. In case he do come back, you think you could train just one of them dogs for use more than kissin visitors to death?"

"How long you reckon before we can relax?"

"Till we die or he kills us." José smiled.

"I'm gonna miss old Breon a little."

"He woulda stabbed us. He was a killer."

"Don't mean I can't miss 'im," Ray said.

"I'm gonna miss Mr. O," said José.

"Whaddaya mean?"

"First thing I'm gonna do if I'm Breon? I'm gonna lay a bad rap on us, tell Mr. O we was the ones casin the joints."

"Didn't think of that," Ray said.

"You didn't think of much, chuckin a motherfuckin six-thousand-dollar laptop into a river."

"We got to tell Mr. O about Breon."

"By the time we get to Mr. O face-to-face, Breon'll have soured him on us."

"I'll write him a letter then, no return address. I can't believe we'll never see Mr. O again. He was cool."

"He was," José said. "He was a father figurine to me. Ya orphaned me again, Ray. Congratulations. You saved some rich asshole's social security number, and all it cost you was our father, our big brother and our jobs." José chuckled, studied the fake gun in his hand. "You are one lame-ass sonuvabitch."

20

YOLIE SMOOTHED THINGS out with old Romeo, and J again was peddling pie for The Slice Is Right. He and Trini were at it hotter and heavier than ever. Yolie got Ray Mr. Fix-It work around the neighborhood, hired Ray to renovate her attic. "For my niece Vanessa. She coming soon. For a guest room."

Ray knew the guests Yolie wanted. Well, he figured, if I can't live over Yolanda's Braid Palace, I can work here and be near Trini. "Thank you, ma'am. I appreciate the work."

One rainy six o'clock as Ray was leaving The Palace Yolie said, "All that water, chico. You boys should spend the night."

"Nah, thanks, ma'am. I got new tin up on the roof now, we're good."

"You sure? I got a brand-new beautiful guest room upstairs."

Ray had just finished the attic renovation that afternoon. He smiled, appreciative of her compliment. "Thanks, Mom—I mean ma'am, sorry about that."

Yolie pinched his cheek. "Stay for dinner, amor. Let Yolie feed you."

He stayed, chowed home-cooked medianoches Cubanos, hot pressed sandwiches of jamón, roast beef, queso blanco, sweet pickle slathered with a stick of butter cut longwise, folded into a chewy white roll, fried and flattened with a giant clothing iron. Yolie did up the tamale rice and beans twice refried, pan flashed shredded lettuce, green chili sauce top. "Too bad José's workin," Ray said, mouth full. "Maybe I could bring some home for 'im?"

"Ob'course." Yolie watched Ray eat. "Nice to cook for a man again. Please, amor, have more, have more."

"José's not workin tonight," Trini said. "Said he had to meet a friend."

"First I heard," Ray said. What trouble you getting us into now, partner?

Dishes done, Ray and Trini tried to figure out how to send pictures from her new mobile phone to her computer. "Vanny called last night. She says she can't wait to meet you."

Ray smiled. Lately he was working hard to convince himself this thing with Trini's cousin was going to work out.

Trini nudged him. "You two are gonna—"

"Trinita amor," Yolie called from downstairs. "Help Yolie brush el Gordito. I hold him, you brush. Bring me my leather gloves."

Trini down with Yolie and the screaming cat, Ray went through the pictures on Trini's phone, found one of José and Trini, their arms around each other, cheek to cheek, big smiles. They were perfect together, sickeningly perfect.

Ray made a gangster face, took a picture of himself, figured out how to e-mail that one and the rest of the pix to Trini's computer.

Trini came back, stalled behind Ray as he fiddled with her computer, massaged his shoulders, rested her hand on his neck. "How's it goin?"

At her touch he almost reached up and took her hand. He didn't. He clicked her laptop's desktop. The screen's wallpaper was the cute picture of Trini and the J-man.

"Cool!" Trini said. She slapped Ray's shoulder. "Tt, doesn't have a phone, doesn't have a computer, he figures it out. How?"

Ray shrugged. "He can read directions."

VROOM-VROOM! "Yo Trini!" came from the street. *VROOM-VROOOOOM!*

They looked out the window.

Down in the late-day street, the rain long gone, José saddled a big old junker of a Kawasaki motorcycle. His collar flipped up, he wore a beat-to-hell leather jacket, the coolest Ray had ever seen.

"Oh my God," Trini said. "He did it."

"Come on, y'all. Check it out!"

They ran down to the street. Yolie was already out there, lecturing José to be careful. "Where's your helmet?"

He grabbed it from the back of the bike seat, slipped it over Trini's head.

"You did not steal this bike, please tell me," Trini said.

"Bought and paid for, every dollar from pedalin Slice Is Right."

"Then I'll ride it."

"You sure will." He grabbed her around the waist, swung her onto the seat behind him. "Hang on, baby. She don't look like much, but she can fly." He pulled back on the throttle, let out the brake, and they did fly, Trini wrapped around him, clinging to break bones, both screaming laughter.

"Ten cuidado!" Yolie called after them. "They gonna kill themselves. Madre de Dios, he is movie star gorgeous on that bike, though."

Ray nodded, smiled, died a little more.

Next round was Yolie's, Yolie so scared she kept her eyes closed, her face hidden in the J-man's back. "Slow down! Oh my God! Coño, hombre, slow *down*!" she laughed.

José slow-rolled her and still she screamed. He let her off in front of the shop, gunned up the street alone, gunned back, popped and rode a wheelie the length of the block, no helmet, long 'rows flying, his smile brighter than the sun splash on the street windows.

"Ohmygodohmygodohmygod!" Trini said. She was trembling, crying, laughing. She took a picture of José with her phone, ran into the shop.

"Where you going?" Yolie said.

"*Tengo que* e-mail *esta a mis chicas!* They gonna die."

Yolie winked. "Gonna be a lot a slippery panties in the Heights tonight, eh, Raymundo chico?" She covered her mouth, laughed, embarrassed, slapped Ray's shoulder. "Tt, I can't believe old Yolie said that!"

José skidded up to the shop. "C-mon, Ray-Ray!"

"Nah nah, I'm a'right."

Yolie put the helmet over Ray's head. "It's *fun,* chico. Vayate."

José grabbed Ray by the shirt, jerked him toward the bike. Ray got on, the helmet too small for his monster dome.

José grinned, winked to Yolie. "Don't wait up for us." He rolled back all the way on the throttle, kicked the clutch, popped the break.

The force of the acceleration slammed Ray back to the sissy bar. "Shit."

"Be *care*ful, Josito," Yolie screamed. "Slow down. Slow down!"

◆

They tore it up down by Macombs Dam Bridge on Powell Boulevard, a long run without lights that dead-ended at the Polo Ground Houses. All the bikers came here.

"Serious, you steal it?" Ray yelled to be heard over the wind.

José yelled back, "Tt *no,* man, Frankie the Fence, three hundrit fitty bucks, plus he threw in the jacket."

"Bike's gotta be hotter than a hungry whore."

"What!"

"I said, bike's hot!"

"It sure is. Hang on, son!"

"How you know how to ride so good?"

"Psh, ridin my trick bike is harder. Ray, I been dreamin of this ride since the womb. Man, the wind feels good, huh? Born to ride, baby! HOOOOO*yeah!*"

A cop cruiser picked them up out on the avenue.

"We are so done," Ray said.

"No we ain't."

"You got no helmet, no *license,* hot plates—"

José bobbed and weaved with the cabs, northwest.

"Where you goin?"

"Jersey, man! They ain't chase us over the bridge!"

"Stop, man! I gotta get off! You're goin too fast now!"

"You wanna go to juvie? Then hang on!" José gunned it, ditched one cruiser then another in the traffic. Three minutes later they were on the Trans-Manhattan Expressway, weaving through the fast-moving traffic, gunning it on the shoulder, onto the ramp that swung around to the upper deck of the GW Bridge, one lane blocked with cones and cleared for roadwork. "This is gonna be beautiful. You better hold tight now, Ray!"

"Goddammit, why?"

"We gonna fly now!" José pulled the bike into a slow-rise wheelie. "Like Grand Theft live, baby! Hoo, Ray! Hooooooo!"

"Slow down, man! Put the wheel down, J-man, please! You gonna kill us!"

"Flyin off a bridge on a motorcycle. Pick a better death. Hahahaaaa! Scarface's got you, kid! No harm can come to us! I feel it! We're God's chosen this one minute! Yayuh! They'll never catch us, Ray-Ray! Never! We the Wonder Thieves!"

Ray clung to the J-man, took it all in, the sunset on the bridge, the sky stacked with every shade of red, the Hudson cliffs eternal, the wind cold. Two kids flying on one wheel.

21

COME MAY'S END, Yolie threw Trini an end of the school year party.

The boys grabbed hot showers at the rec center. Ray fussed with his zits in front of the dented metal mirror.

"Stop pickin at 'em, Ray-Ray. You're makin it worse. Chill, son. You act nervous you gonna scare her off."

"I ain't nervous, a'right?"

Trini's cousin Vanny was going to be at the party, fresh off the plane from San Juan.

Ray splashed himself with cheap cologne, passed the bottle to José.

"Man, we smell good, huh?" José said. "Lemme have a little more of that stuff." The J-man splashed his armpits.

Ray copied the J-man.

◆

Yolie's yard was packed with kids from Trini's school. They were okay, better than Ray expected. Some were even nice. The prep school chicks flirted with José as he worked the meat grill, played with his long shiny cornrows, which Yolie and Trini had beaded that morning with Day-Glo red. He was polite but made it known he was Trini's man. Even Yolie mussed his braids at one point. She was a little tipsy on Cuervo. José winked at Trini. She blew him a kiss. He caught it, pasted it onto his lips.

Seeing José like this, a corny family man, Ray figured the J-man and Trini would get married someday. If José didn't get his ass shot off robbing a jewelry store.

Ray was on bun patrol, working the midget grill. Small as it was, it threw heat this hot night. Ray sweat. He looked over to José, shirt off, tied around his waist. Ray stuffed a hotdog bun into his mouth. He was drunk on beer to work up his courage to face Vanessa, due in any minute.

Trini passed a tray of hors d'oeuvres. The late-day light in the yard, Trini glowed. Ray hurt.

Yolie screamed. Trini spun and screamed. They attacked the girl who had just come into the yard, the three ladies kissing. Trini grabbed the girl's hand, lugged her over to Ray. Trini rubbed Ray's shaved head. "Vanita, this is the famous Ray Mond. Raymond, this is my cousin Vanessa."

Vanessa was pudgy, like Ray. She wasn't Trini, but she was all right.

Ray nodded to Vanessa. "Yup," he said. "Hi, I mean. I'm

R—" He stopped saying his name because he remembered Trini had just said his name twice.

Trini pinched Ray's cheek. "Told ya he was funny. Isn't he just adorable, girl?"

Vanessa looked down at her feet, frowned. "I don't know. I better unpack." She went into the braid shop.

Ray nodded. "Yup, she don't like me a half a bit."

"Nah nah, I'm tellin you, boy. Look, she's shy. Give it time, you'll see."

"Yolie, we need more cow." José came out from the kitchen holding up the last bag of burgers, slapped them onto the grill.

Yolie went for her pocketbook.

"I'll go, Yolie," Ray said.

"It's okay, amor," Yolie said. "You stay and have fun."

"I need the air anyhow."

Yolie gave Ray money. "Go to the diner, tell them I sent you. They give you a fifty-pack of burgers."

Ray took the money. "Which diner?"

Trini took Ray's hand. "I'll show you. C'mon."

On the way to the diner they walked one of Trini's guy friends to the subway. The cat kept talking about this girl he was in love with, heartbroken that the chick didn't know he existed. "It's like I'm invisible," he said. Trini comforted the guy, kissed him at the subway steps, told him she would call him tomorrow.

Ray felt bad for the kid, or maybe he just felt bad for himself. "He seems real busted up."

"He's a sweetie, but I tell you, the *drama,* a different crush every week." Trini slugged Ray's shoulder, jumped up and down. "So, Ray, how you feelin about Vanny?"

He was feeling like he had stomach cancer. "Seems real sweet."

"I just think you two are the perfect match, you know?"

"How's that?"

"You're both so nice."

Fat, you mean. "Thanks."

"You wanna double tomorrow, you, me, Vanny and the J-man, hit the zoo?" The sunset bouncing off the shop windows painted Trini gold, her teeth bright against her tanned face, her eyes dark fire.

"I love you," Ray said.

"What?" Trini said.

Ray cleared his throat, hoped he didn't look as sick as he felt. "I'd love to. The zoo. Sounds great."

He wiped the sweat off his face with his shirt, gut hanging.

"Ray? Baby, what's wrong?"

She called me baby. He smiled, winked, more like blinked, Ray a lousy winker. "Let's get the meat."

"Dude, Xbox *so* thrashes PlayStation."

"Dude? That's like saying Pac-Man *so* thrashes Grand Theft Auto?"

"Dude, why do you say everything like it's a question?"

"I so do not?"

The kids from Trini's school sat in a circle, smoking cigarettes. Ray, José, and Trini watched from the picnic table. Yolie had gone to bed. Vanessa never came back out to the party. She kept looking out the back window of the attic apartment to see if Ray was still there. He waved to her once, but she backed away from the window fast without waving back.

Trini and José held hands as they shared a beer. Ray had his own beer. He was bombed.

"No, dude, seriously, am I right or am I right?"

"Dude, I am so not getting involved in this one?"

Trini looked at José. "Whattaya think?"

José sipped his beer. "I think one more dude, we got us a rodeo."

"Y'all wanna call party over and bounce? Raymond?"

"Yeah. T, you think it's okay we take the burnt food for the dogs?"

"We'll take all of it, burnt and non-burnt," she said.

"They'll like that."

"They'll like any dag thing," José said. "My beautiful dogs." José winked at Ray.

Trini rolled her eyes, pinched the J-man's arm. "Lemme go see if Vanny wants to come."

"Nah, T, don't push her," Ray said.

"Raymond, don't be like that. She's sick from too much Dramamine, she told me."

"Dramamine. Right."

"To make her be chill on the plane."

"Nah, nah, leave her," Ray said. "Let her rest."

"Quit bein a baby about it," José said. "Just let Trini go on up—"

"*No* man, and shut *up,* callin me a baby."

"A'right, a'right now," Trini said, "let's not pressure the man. Tomorrow y'all come on up here for lunch with the motorcycle, we'll get her into the swing."

"The goddam motorcycle," Ray muttered. "Right."

"Ray," Trini said. "What is the *matter,* chico mio? Tt, talk to us."

"You okay, Ray-Ray?"

He looked at them, saw their confusion, their concern for him, looked away, felt his eyes brim.

Three kids from Trini's school started shoving a fourth kid.

"You two big strong boys help me clear these dudes out of my aunt's yard," Trini said.

They did.

22

THEY WENT TO Ten Mile River. Ray hung out back with the dogs and read by flashlight while Trini and José hung out in front of the TV. Ray could see them through the window but they couldn't see him because the light was on inside the house. Ray couldn't help staring. He watched José kiss Trini's neck. José slinked his hand up the inside of Trini's leg into her skirt, she pushed it away. "No, baby," she said. "*No.* Be a good boy." They went back to kissing. José clicked off the light, only TV flicker now, not enough to spy by.

Ray got back to his book as he fed the dogs leftovers. Aristotle told him that a man who couldn't live in society was either a beast or god. "Does he have to be one or the other, Fatty?"

Fatty stared at Ray out the sides of his eyes.

"Dammit, José, I said no." Trini's voice louder now. "Why can't you be nice?"

"I'm tryin a be nice," José said. "Tryin a make you feel nice."

"I feel fine, thank you. You behave, Mr. Man."

It was quiet for a while, then José said, "I'm sorry, baby. C'mere."

Ray hugged the Fatty dog. Fatty yawned to show his toothless mouth.

"José! I'm serious! Y'all quit it!"

"I'll kill him," Ray whispered to Fatty.

"C'mon, Trini," José said. "I'm a man, see. A man got needs."

Ray stood. His stomach was hot with sloshing beer.

"José!" Trini said.

Ray thought, You better stop, José. Then he thought, You better stop José.

"Wait," Trini yelled.

Ray looked up. The stars over Ten Mile River spun.

"*Stop,* please!"

There was the sound of a hand slapping a face. The dogs gathered at Ray's feet, cocked their ears.

Ray stumbled around to the front of the stationhouse. By the time he got there, Trini and José were on their feet. José had his hand to his cheek. Trini said, "You had to ruin it, huh? We were having a nice night, and you had to get all . . . Yo, I am out."

"Good, go." José threw his beer bottle at the wall. It smashed and sprayed dregs and glass. "Goddam. I didn't mean that." He put his hands out to Trini to make peace. "Trini, man. I'm sorry."

Trini pulled away.

"Trin—" José said.

Ray grabbed José's arm.

"Ray, man, leggo my damn arm now. This ain't none of your concern, son."

"Raymond—" Trini said.

"What you done to her?" Ray said.

"I ain't done *nothin,* okay? Jesus. Now lemme *go.*"

"Okay, look," Trini said. "Let's all just *calm* down, okay?"

"Ray, easy, boss," José said. "I was, I lost it for a second. *Chill.*"

"You don't mess with a chick like that," Ray said. "Even I know that. No is no."

"I know. I—"

"You don't know *shit.*"

"I'm-a warn you a last time, son, get out my face, pissin me right off. You keep steppin to me, you'll pay the devil with bright red blood."

"Y'all quit it!" Trini said.

"Ha," Ray said. "*I'm*-a pay the devil?

José shoved Ray off.

"Stop!" Trini said.

Ray slipped on the neck of the broken beer bottle, went down hard.

"Raymond? You okay, sweetie pie?" Trini helped Ray up.

José paced and tugged his braids. "Dag, see what you made me do? Aw, hell, Ray. Hell." He went to help Ray up.

Ray pushed past Trini, drove his rock of a fist into José's face. José got his hand up, deflected some of the punch but not enough. His head snapped back.

A click.

José hit the floor like a sack of wet trash dropped from a second-floor window.

No sooner had Ray tagged José than he wished he had no hands to hit with.

Ray and Trini stood over José. The J-man's head was twisted so that he was looking over his shoulder, except he wasn't looking at anything because his eyes were closed.

Trini backed away from Ray, bent to José. "José? José! No. No."

The dogs had come in. They sniffed at José. When they saw he wasn't moving their hackles went up. They backed out of the stationhouse, eyes on Ray, bolted when they hit the woods. Only the Fatty dog was left. He stared at José out of the side of his eyes. Then he turned to face Ray head-on. The dog shivered and slinked out, bumping into everything in its blindness.

Ray called after the dog, "Fatty, c'mere."

The dog bolted at the sound of Ray's voice and disappeared into the darkness.

Ray and Trini dragged José to the junky old couch. He was breathing. They sat him up so he wouldn't swallow the blood in his mouth. Ray kept saying sorry. Sometimes José would shake his head, sometimes nod.

Trini turned away, her face in her hands. "Y'all boys. Y'all poor boys. Oh my God. The air in here," she cried softly, more to herself than to them. "The godawful stale air. The dust and damp and mold rot in the walls. Look at this place," she whispered. "Dog hair everywhere. I'm so sorry. I must have been out of my mind. This is my fault."

"Hell you talkin about, T?" José was coming around. "You didn't do anything."

"That's right. I didn't. Look at you boys. Y'all aren't thirty-two yet, your ages added, and you're stone drunk. Y'all smoke and steal and fight." Trini took out her phone, battery dead. "Shit."

"Who you callin?" Ray said.

"I need a cab," she said.

"We'll walk you home," José said.

"No! No you will not. I can't be around you boys right now. Y'all make me so sad and mad and I don't know, I just don't know." Trini closed her eyes, grimaced. "I hate myself." She got up, ran out of the stationhouse.

"Lemme get her to a cab, be back," Ray said to José.

"Don't let her walk them woods alone." Unable to stand José collapsed into the couch.

Ray caught up with Trini on a section of Drive filled with old folks a-stroll in the warm May night. "Get away from me," she said to Ray.

"T, yo, I'm sorry," Ray said.

"Get away. Every step you take toward me, I scream." And she did. "Get! A! Way! From! Me!"

Folks stopped, stared.

"Leave me alone, Raymond. Leave me be." She hurried down the Drive.

Ray stopped chasing her, roared beer puke into the bushes.

Ray stepped it back to the stationhouse, relieved to find José on his feet, making coffee. "She's okay?" José said.

"I don't know about that."

"You got puke on your shirt." José sipped hot coffee. "Phew."

"I don't know what to say, J-man."

"Don't say sorry. I hate that."

"I know."

"You did the right thing. I was outta line. I tell you though, son, that was some punch. Think m' blockin hand's a little messed up."

"Lemme take you to Doc."

"Nah, don't hurt much. Prob'ly bad sprained. We'll

see how she plays tomorrow." José chugged the coffee, rubbed his throat. "M'damn neck smarts more than my face. Whiplash. My eye's a-swellin, ain't she? I feel it puf-fin to blind me."

"I'll fetch some ice."

"Nah, I like it like this." He checked himself out in his shaving mirror. "Looks cool."

Ray scanned the trashed stationhouse, broomed the bottle glass, worried the dogs would cut their feet. Then a worse fear came to him: The dogs weren't coming back. He heard one of them barking, far away.

"Damn, I love that girl, though," José said. "I hope I didn't mess up permanent."

"Get her some flowers."

"Know where I could get some nice flowers this hour, partner?"

"Deli."

"Right." José swiped a breath, threw his arm over Ray's shoulder. "Pal o' mine, I'm skunk drunk."

"Thankfully. Otherwise your face would hurt a ton."

"Prob'ly hurt a ton tomorrow, huh? Coffee's startin to kick in though. I'm gonna be jacked up enough to puke in a minute. Let's go get Trini. I got some apologizin to do."

"You do. You go. I'll stay here, sweep up, whistle the dogs back."

"Leave 'em. Hell, I'm trying to dump 'em all these years,

and now you're gonna whistle 'em back? 'Sides, you can't even whistle."

"Imagine Breon came back right now, no dogs to warn us?" Ray said, face blank.

"Son, Breon comes back now, he can have me. I'm ready for the bullet. I ain't felt this whipped since juvie. You go get the damn dogs, I'll get Trini, we'll all meet back here in half a hour, make us some more coffee and play poker." José jabbed Ray's arm as he limped for the door on woozy legs. At the door, he spun around, suddenly wide-awake. "Ray, quick, out the back way, run."

"Huh?"

"Cops!" José pushed Ray outside. "Run, man!"

Ray ran for the weed tree forest. Then it hit him: Trini had run south. Yolie's was north, south was the precinct. He spun around. José had tripped twenty yards back. He waved Ray on. "Git, man," he wheezed.

Ray pulled José into the weed tree thickets, threw José's arm over his shoulder. They limped as one by moonshine.

José pulled away, out of breath. "I ain't-a make it, man. My head, man, gonna explode. I'm shit dizzy. *Go*."

"I ain't ditchin you."

"Then we split up. Meet in that dead spot there under the highway, that street that runs—duck."

Flashlights swept the trees.

"Okay, listen a me, Ray-Ray. Here's what we do. Go to the dock. Boost a skiff. River's dark as hell. They won't see you on the water once you get past the sewage plant there. You know what I'm talking about?"

"Yeah, but hell with that, I ain't leavin you behind."

"Right right, I know I know, but you're gonna get the boat, right? Then I'll *mee*t you, see?"

"You're lyin a me."

"Goddammit, son! I ain't lyin! You pick me up on the other side of the plant, a'right? You go the long way for the boat, take the tracks. I'll shortcut by the overpass. I won't make it if I go the long way. I see you in ten minutes." José limped back toward the stationhouse.

"You're snowin me bad, man."

"I'll meet you. And brother? Once you hit them tracks, you run. Now git." José limped away onto the trail.

Flashlights hit José. He cupped his hands, yelled south instead of where Ray would run, north, "Run, Ray!"

One of the cops jumped at the decoy, ran south.

José screamed south, "They're comin, Ray!"

Another cop went south.

A third cop cuffed José. José didn't fight. He screamed, "Run! Run."

Ray squeezed through the rip in the chain link, slid down the weed-struck wall onto the tracks. He ran north, hugged the lee wall, tripped in the wall's shadows as he made his way through the trackside trash to the old car, the safe place.

The car had been trashed and ransacked, the backseat

ripped out, the cooler full of canned goods and water emptied. Ray reached under what was left of the dashboard, through the rusted plate that separated the engine from the passenger compartment.

The old pool stick case was still there.

Ray emptied its goods into his pockets, four hundred some dollars of small bills double wrapped in Ziploc, a first aid kit, and a pair of mini binoculars. Wet from old rain the first aid kit was useless but for the brandy flask. Ray pitched the med kit, tucked the flask into his pocket, grabbed the binoculars and slinked through the junkyard south into the wildwood west of the tracks.

From the darkness of the high grass Ray glassed the view uphill on Riverside Drive. The binoculars were funky with dirt in one lens and a crack in the other, but Ray made out Trini's face all right, her hands over her mouth.

The cops walked José past Trini. The J-man begged the cops to let Trini come to him. They did. He kissed her. The cops led him away. Trini was shaking. "I'm sorry, baby," she yelled. "I'm sorry."

Marched halfway up the block José spun back toward Trini, "I *love* you, baby!" He grinned as the cops put him into the back of their cruiser. "I'll be back, baby. Don't worry, darlin, I'll be back."

23

RAY WAITED THREE hours in the high grass until he was sure 5-O wasn't coming back. Ten minutes after the NYPD cruiser drove José away the cops who chased south came back up the Drive, got into their squad car and left. Nothing happened since. Ray spent the better part of those three hours looking for the dogs, gone.

He wondered if he should turn himself in, get back into the system with José. For parole violation they would eat six months, nine max. After that they would be at large once again. Ten Mile was done now that the cops knew about it, but they could head north, find a squat in The Bronx, live free, just like the old days. All he had to do was walk up that hill.

The old days.

No.

Drunk was better than hungover so he kept drinking, slugged from the brandy flask as he pushed through the weed trees toward the water. He hurt at the idea of Fatty on his own. The lame old half-blind mutt would be food for the other dogs soon.

He picked the lock chaining a rowboat to the dock, set the boat in the water, rowed mid river, let the boat coast south.

He snapped the string necklace that kept a spoon at his heart, held the spoon to the sky, told himself that if the spoon bent there was a God, one who had his back. He concentrated as never before but couldn't bend the spoon. He chucked it over the side.

He made himself still to take it in, the fact that he was alone, no man's slave, no man's boss, no man's sidekick.

He wondered about that night out on the river, in these very waters. The blue folks twisted in that suicide embrace on the basement floor, transported over the ice to what he at the time thought was a peaceful end but now knew was no different than leaving them to rot in a dark cellar. They would have decayed either way.

Most of all he wondered about Trini. She'd three times called him Ray instead of Raymond. Tonight she'd called him baby. What might have happened if he never set her up with José, instead plain old asked her out a few times, brought her a few more flowers, told her how he really felt? Would they have had a shot? Last year he would have said no way. But tonight he was thinking maybe. Not yes. Maybe.

He could ride on maybe for a while.

Maybe he would go back to school someday. Maybe he'd be a teacher. Maybe he'd never go back. Maybe he'd be his own teacher, his own student. He didn't know which way he would end up, but—for the first time—he had a hunch he would end up.

The boat slowed, stopped. The tide had gone slack. From the middle of the river Ray saw the light had died out in the empty stationhouse. Now there was nothing left. No José, no Trini, no dogs. Just Ray and Ten Mile River.

Out on the water the air was too damp for a man to take off his shirt, but Ray took off his shirt anyway. He sank the oars and pulled. Rowing south he watched the George Washington Bridge fade in the distance.

"The Wonder Thieves. Yeah, that was us."

Working the boat downriver toward the bay and beyond the bay the ocean, Ray rowed against the tide.

THANK YOU . . .

My wife and life Risa Morimoto, Elisa Paik, Kirby Kim, David Vigliano,

Team Dial, Lauri Hornik, Regina Castillo, Christian Fünfhausen, Jasmin Rubero, Emily Heddleson, Shelley Diaz and especially la reina, Nan Mercado, and the absolutely wonderful Robyn Meshulam,

Scott Smith, Diana Choi, Dave Starr, Quang Bao, Jennifer Carlson, Nan Talese, Jennifer Joel, Nicole Aragi, Nat Sobel, Hammad Zaidi, Cherry Montejo and Eric Chinski,

Sue Lee, Tom Lino, Bobby Wong, Mike Marotta, Tony Capone, Nina Waechter, Francisco Aliwalas, Mike Brisciana, the Central Park Medical Unit, everyone who reached out to the LaMastas, and especially Thommy Garvey,

Rubén Austria and Manthia Henriquez for those remarkable workshops,

Linda Zimmerman, Lisa Watson, Zach Minor, Leticia Guillory, Linda Gomez, George Dick and Gwen Hardwick for a great year with CAT/CRTD,

Luigi Santiago, RIP,

my families, Griffins, Zancas, LaMonicas, Murrays, Fitzgeralds, Morimotos, Imuras, Yamadas, Sakurais and Hoests, especially Kari,

all my goddam dogs,

Johngie, Kath, Matt and the gals,

my mothers, Noriko and the one and only MLG,

AND

my father. Pop, you are the king.

AND

the kids I met teaching: may your courage set you free the way it did me.

Turn the page for a glimpse
of Paul Griffin's acclaimed novel

The Orange Houses

chapter 1
TAMIKA

Bronx West, a high school classroom, a late October Thursday morning twenty-seven days before the hanging . . .

Everybody's eyes were like, Say *what*?

The teacher said the word again: "Taphophobia."

Spelling bee. Hate It scale rating: somewhere between scrubbing toilets and PMS, say 8 out of 10. The big-boned girl in the corner did not speak in front of crowds. She would write her answer on the board or be dumb. She studied the shapes made by old lady Rodriguez's mouth: Ta. Fo. Fo. Bee-ya.

Meningitis struck her ten years before, when she was five. Technically her hearing loss was "moderately severe," what lawyers looking to sue hospitals pegged 50 percent deficient. Being halfway to sound was like never being able to catch your breath.

She got by just fine when she kept her hearing aids turned on. She didn't much. The machines were what City Services could give her, old technology that jug-handled her ears and rattled her with phone and radio static, a high-pitched whir. They sharpened and dulled everything at the same time the way water will just below the surface. But turned off and plugging up her drums, the aids screened out the world. She lived for this silky silence.

"I seen more activity at sleep clinics," Teach said. "Somebody stand and deliver. Mika Sykes, save us."

Tamika rolled her eyes. *Meek*-a? Call her Mik, like *nick*.

Her thick hip caught a desk corner as she hopped over the outstretched foot of the pretty girl Shanelle just back from juvie. Word was Sha kept a box cutter tucked into her sock, its blade home-ground plastic to sneak it through the metal detector but sharp enough to slash and spill some gal's cowhide backpack last week.

Mik stabbed the blackboard with fresh chalk and spun back to her seat. She propped her head on stacked fists and closed her eyes. She was up late again last night doing her secret thing, slinking away into her dream world: drawing. Add to the no-sleep night a sugar hangover to pound the gray out of her dome. She'd washed down a box of Fig Newtons with a snuck beer. Eyes shut she saw what she drilled into the slate:

TAPHOPHOBIA
FEAR OF BEING BURIED ALIVE

At lunch another outcast bum-rushed her loner spot under the stairs. The G he called himself. So sad. He handed Mik his homework. Mik eyed the paper, algebra, held up three fingers.

"For ten questions?" The dude fished his pockets and came up with lint and dirty pennies. "All I got is a buck and some."

Mik squinted, taking in The G. Thick glasses bugged his eyes. A mouthful of metal failed to tame his buckteeth. That twisting sting pitted her stomach: repulsion, lust, both. She had a thing for losers. She grabbed the coins.

"Yo, I like y'all's braids bunched like that," he said. "Cat's ears is crazy sexy."

Mom had rolled them that morning as Mik ate breakfast—an annoying ritual. Mik fought a blush as she flipped up her phone. She clicked a hot key for a ready reply text: WUT EVR.

"Mik, lemme watch you do it, the math."

Another hot key: NOT NEVR. Last time she let him watch he faked a yawn and dropped his arm over her shoulder. So corny. She had let him brush her breast, his hand clammy and shaking. That was either too disgusting or too exciting, and she'd nailed him, elbow to ribs.

"Y'all are mad beautiful."

"Y'all are blind." The words were out before she realized she spoke them. She sounded twice as good as she thought she did, half as good as she thought she should. With her ears plugged her voice was a hollow echo trapped in her head. Stick your fingers in your ears and talk, you'll get the idea.

"Same way, slip it through my locker slot, text me after you make the drop?"

That got the BET button. She watched the player wannabe pimp limp away. Sucker would get his fool butt shot off during some bagman errand—a corpse before he hit the right to enlist. Mik blinked away that sadness and checked the boy's math. G did not stand for genius. Poor baby, she almost said.

Doing other kids' homework for small change wasn't glamorous, but she had her eye on this dope ergonomic pen that cost forty-six bucks at that Japanese bookstore downtown. She worked old-school style with Speedball ink and crow quill points. She did not dare dream the pen could be more than a hobby piece, maybe even her ticket out, a one-way escape from Mom's fate: slaving behind the Dunkin' Donuts counter when she wasn't humping the overnight restock shift at Target.

She tucked The G's buck-and-some into her pocket and started in on his algebra. The half-off discount was no sweat. She helped out when she could, but on the down low, no need to get friendly. She'd do a slow kid's math or help a blind lady cross a street. Hit and run, over and done, like that. She didn't know why she did these things. They didn't make her feel good. They didn't make her feel bad either. She couldn't figure it out.

She pulled her hair out of the bunched braids to hide her ears.

chapter 2 FATIMA

Atlantic Ocean, five miles southeast of New York Harbor, Friday, twenty-six days before the hanging, 3 a.m. . . .

"Don't be afraid," the ship's mate said from the hatchway above. "Come."

The women tiptoed onto the deck as if they were treading landmined sands. For nine days they had been hiding in the backup engine room of this oil tanker fit for hauling two million barrels of light sweet crude and, this time around, thirty-four refugees. Each woman's passage cost twenty-five hundred dollars. This blind faith cash had been raised a coin at a time, person by displaced person, family by fractured African family. Those who had endured were sending their best shots at survival, if not by bloodline then heritage, west.

Of the thirty-four, most were going to Camden, where

the Immigration police did not go. Camden was written off as a city lost to drugs, prostitution and the nation's highest teen mortality rate. The rest of these travelers were going to a city somewhat safer yet no less rife with illegal employment, Atlantic City. The rest save Fatima Espérer.

Her mother had given the young woman her first name, but for her new life Fatima chose the last, a French word meaning to hope. She taught herself the language from schoolbooks that somehow escaped burning—English too. At sixteen she was headed where all told her not to go: New York. She had to visit the Statue of Liberty.

"A silly tourist trap," one of her sister travelers said.

Fatima smiled. Trap or not, she was going to see Liberty up close.

The refugees huddled at the bow, their shawls drawn tight around their heads and shoulders. The ship's mate ordered the deck lights turned off. He pointed overhead.

Fatima looked up. The night sky swung as the freighter wrestled a broken wave. The stars were nearly the same ones she saw back home before the raids, the fires, the smoke. On the horizon were the lights of Brooklyn, Staten Island, Manhattan and somewhere in the glow the Great Lady. Fatima leaned on a somewhat friend's shoulder. "If we see only this, the trip was worth it."

The other woman furled her lips and eyes as she relit a half cigarette she'd earned by way of a grabby kiss with a mechanic. "If I see only this, I want my goddamned money back."

chapter 3 TAMIKA

Courtyard of a Bronx West housing project, Saturday, twenty-five days before the hanging, 6:30 p.m. . . .

The Orange Houses were not orange. They were beaten brick the color of the sky this drizzly dusk. Some long-dead architect Casper Orange slapped together the nine jail-like towers way back when. Small, deep-set windows grayed cinderblock hallways noisy with need.

Mik hustled her grocery bags into tower #4 to beat the rain. The elevator was grounded again. After a ten-flight hike up the fire stairs she found NaNa passed out on the couch. Tostitos Natural Blue crumbs buckshot the old woman's chest. Nosebleed channel TV teased with an info-mercial for an exercise machine nobody could afford. The floor vibrated with the TV's fake enthusiasm jacked all the way up. NaNa was not Deaf, but old-lady deaf. *Wha*jou say? *Wha*jou call me?

The woman had no folks, but everybody called her NaNa because she would sit your kid for a free meal. If you left a beer or two in the fridge for her, that was fine too. Going on three years now Mik and Mom didn't have the heart to tell the old gal she wasn't needed anymore.

Mik clicked to MTV to taunt herself. Some cutie was getting down with a guitar.

She put her hand on the TV speaker. Slow-strummed chords buzzed her fingertips and triggered a memory of Mom working that big body acoustic gathering closet dust the last ten years.

She clicked on her hearing aids. The music was ruined in them, the notes crackly edges and angles. Outside her window the city thumped with the coming night crowd: sellers, buyers, screamers, liars. In the background NaNa snored to cure comas.

Mik clicked off her aids.

This was what it was all about—the sadness muted. She could live and die without hearing another people-made noise. Except that guitar.

She changed the channel to the news. Closed captions flashed. HOUSE OVERRIDES PREZ'S VETO. CONTROVERSIAL IMMIGRATION BILL MOVES TO SENATE. BILL OFFERS REWARD $ TO ENCOURAGE REPORTING OF ILLEGALS.

Mik had enough problems without worrying about Mexicans stealing Americans' delivery bike jobs. She aimed the clicker, killed the TV and tucked a blanket around NaNa. Sure the old gal was asleep, Mik pecked a kiss onto that brow lined with seventy-some years of disappointment. She went to her room and pulled a throwaway briefcase from her closet. Inside were sketchbooks, pens and inks of all colors.

She kept the briefcase hidden behind her off-season threads. In her mind she heard Mom: *Why you spending all that time drawing instead of studying? You make all A's, you get yourself a free ride to college. You wanna end up like me, double shifting Target and Dunkin's? My daughter gonna end up slinging Hennessey cocktails at Applebee's for thug pimps, blah, blah, blah . . .*

Moms, Moms, Moms . . . How I want to love you.

Who wanted to go to college? After X463, aka Bronx-Orange high school, yo, Mik was *out*.

What then?

Whatever.

She studied her sketches. Cityscapes to the last one, they were remarkable, odd, the world a century after the plague. Buildings miraculously defied decay beneath gorgeous skies, no one around to enjoy them. Her streets were empty.

She checked her ink bottles. She was out of the most important color, the bones of every drawing, black. She tucked the briefcase into its hiding spot and crashed facedown into sheets that needed washing.

Don't miss Paul Griffin's